The Adventures of Dirt Clod
and his sidekick Bird Bones

STU STORIES

The Adventures of Dirt Clod
and his sidekick Bird Bones

Patrick "Bird Bones" Hueller
with illustrations by Adam Record

SWEETWATER
BOOKS

An Imprint of Cedar Fort, Inc.
Springville, Utah

This is a work of fiction. The characters, names, incidents, places, and dialogue are products of the author's imagination, and are not to be construed as real. The views expressed within this work are the sole responsibility of the author and do not necessarily reflect the position of Cedar Fort, Inc., or any other entity.

ISBN 13: 978-1-4621-1955-4

Published by Sweetwater Books, an imprint of Cedar Fort, Inc., 2373 W. 700 S., Springville, UT 84663
Distributed by Cedar Fort, Inc., www.cedarfort.com

LIBRARY OF CONGRESS CATALOGING-IN-PUBLICATION DATA

Names: Hueller, Patrick, 1983- author.
Title: Stu stories / Patrick Hueller.
Description: Springville, Utah : Sweetwater Books, An imprint of Cedar Fort, Inc., [2017]
Identifiers: LCCN 2016030210 | ISBN 9781462119554 (perfect bound : alk. paper)
Subjects: LCSH: Junior high school boys--Fiction. | LCGFT: Short stories.
Classification: LCC PS3608.U349627 S78 2016 | DDC 813/.6--dc23
LC record available at https://lccn.loc.gov/2016030210

Cover design by M. Shaun McMurdie
Illustrations by Adam Record
Cover design © 2017 by Cedar Fort, Inc.
Edited and typeset by Jessica Romrell and Erica Myers

Printed in the United States of America

10 9 8 7 6 5 4 3 2 1

Printed on acid-free paper

For the real Stu.

"The more legendary this book becomes, the more legendary I become."
–Stu

"Stu and Bird Bones' adventures are hilarious, sometimes horrifying, and definitely legendary. This book hits on pretty much every topic I cared about when I was a kid (love, Jedis, severed legs, etc.)."
–Geoff Herbach, author of *Fat Boy vs. the Cheerleaders*

"Because I'm Patrick 'Bird Bones' Hueller's brother, people ask me, 'Did everything in Stu Stories really happen?' But enough about Patrick. Let's get back to talking about me."
–Andy Hueller, author of *Skipping Stones at the Center of the Earth* and other amazing books

"Really fun . . . has tones of *Wayside School* and *Maniac Magee* and *How Angel Peterson Got His Name*."
–Kurtis Scaletta, author of *Mudville*

"Stu Stories captures eighth-grade life in its finest and wackiest form. A fun-filled zany ride!"
–Frank Cole, author of *The Afterlife Academy*

CONTENTS

Dear Reader,

There are two things you need to know about my childhood friend Stu Sanderson. The first is that he was tall. Really, really tall. By eighth grade he was close to seven feet tall.

The second? His goal in life was to be legendary.

Sincerely,

Patrick "Bird Bones" Hueller

Stu Sanderson Vanishes in the Middle of Class

Ms. Gribbs was Stu's and my eighth-grade English teacher. She had thin lips that she smeared too much lipstick on and frizzy hair that she piled on top of her head.

The other thing you need to know about Ms. Gribbs is that, well, to use the technical term, the woman was batty.

I mean this with all due respect, but she was a total nut job.

We're talking Loony Tunes here.

I'm not saying this to be cruel. I actually liked Ms. Gribbs a lot. But that doesn't change the fact that her brain was seriously warped.

For instance, she made us sit in a circle every day.

Okay, that might not sound so crazy. You might have even had classes where you sat in a circle.

But if you did, I bet those classes didn't have thirty-eight kids in them.

Don't get me wrong. Her reason for making us sit in a circle was noble. If I remember right, it had something to do with King Arthur. He supposedly had a round table so everyone felt equally involved in whatever was going on. Which is what Ms. Gribbs said she wanted too. Equality.

Cool idea, right?

One problem: we didn't fit in a circle. Not really. The only way Ms. Gribbs could squeeze us all in was to push the desks really close to the walls. One of the desks sat right in front of the door. We actually had to climb over it in order to enter or exit the classroom. Even then we didn't quite fit. Ms. Gribbs had to scooch her own desk—yep, she sat in a student desk as well—slightly inside the circle.

Which is why Stu volunteered to sit right next to her.

At first, I didn't get it. Why would someone who aimed to make mischief want to sit so close to the teacher? Everyone knows the more mischief one plans to make, the farther he or she should sit from the teacher.

"You don't understand, Bird Bones," Stu said to me at lunch. Bird Bones was his nickname for me.

"Understand what?" I asked.

"The paradigm has shifted, dude."

He really talked like that. Lots of *dudes*. Lots of big words like *paradigm*.

To this day I don't know where he came up with these words.

"Now that Ms. G's got us in a circle," he continued, "the best way to get off her radar is to get out of her peripherals, dude. The closer I sit, the easier it is to do that."

As usual, Stu was right.

To prove it, he routinely got out of his desk without Ms. Gribbs noticing. Usually, he would just pace the front of the room, one long stride at a time. He'd go from the file cabinet, past the chalkboard, to the podium Ms. Gribbs had tucked away in the other corner. After touching the podium, he'd pivot around and head back.

Back and forth, back and forth.

Then, one day, he stopped.

Stopped pacing. Stopped dead in his tracks.

He was right behind Ms. Gribbs, and he stood there like that, towering over her, apparently deep in thought. He scratched his chin with his long fingers, and then—finally—nodded his head as though he'd made a decision.

He took a long step backward and began walking sideways. His shoulder blades smeared the chalk on the blackboard as he moved.

When he got to the podium, he stopped again.

There must have been some space between the podium and the wall—but it couldn't have been much. Then again, Stu never needed much space. He may have been unbelievably tall, but he was also unbelievably skinny. The expression "paper thin" comes to mind.

In fact, that's a perfect way to describe him in that moment.

I don't know exactly how he did it, but in one stepping, twisting, contorting motion, Stu managed to fold himself up like origami until he was *inside* the podium.

It had never occurred to me that the podium was hollow, so Stu's disappearance looked like a magic trick.

He'd hunched and bent over and then—all at once—gone, *poof!*

At some point, Ms. Gribbs turned to check on Stu. After all the times she'd caught him pacing back and forth, swiveling her head around had become like a nervous tic.

When she didn't see Stu in his desk, she swiveled her head some more.

When she didn't see Stu pacing, well . . .

Remember what I said about her being—to use proper terminology—completely cracked?

Ms. Gribbs didn't turn to us and ask us what Stu had done now. She didn't say, "Okay, Stu—this isn't funny. Get back here this instant." Nope—doing those things would have been too reasonable.

Instead, Ms. Gribbs *shrieked*. "STU!" she shrieked. "WHERE ARE YOU?"

She kept shrieking as she jumped out of her desk. "STUART SANDERSON? ARE YOU THERE?"

She started frantically looking everywhere for him. And I mean everywhere. Under backpacks. Under stacks of paper. Justin Richards had left a mini candy bar wrapper next to him, and Ms. Gribbs picked it up as though Stu might have been hiding under there.

The only place she didn't look was in the podium. It had probably never occurred to her that it was hollow on the inside, either.

The whole time she looked she kept shrieking.

"STU? STU! STU?" she shrieked, climbing the desk in front of the door and leaving the classroom.

The door shut behind her, but there were two panes of glass on either side of it, and we watched her storm up and down the hallway, still shrieking away: "STUART! HELLO? WHERE DID YOU GO?"

Then she was back in the classroom. Her office was in the back corner, and Ms. Gribbs made a beeline for it. She picked up her office phone, punched in some numbers, and yelled, "Principal Davis? Is that you? I'm calling to report a missing student! Repeat: I have a missing student!"

While Ms. Gribbs was still wailing into the phone, Stu unfolded himself and sat back in his desk. He waited calmly for her to come back into the classroom. When she did, he just said, "'Sup, Ms. G?" as though everything was totally normal.

I've thought about this memory for years, and I've never been able to come up with a lesson or moral, other than "insane people act insane sometimes."

Then again, Stu never agreed with my assessment of Ms. Gribbs.

"Insane, Bird Bones? *Ms. G*? No way, dude."

I asked him what else he would call her freak-out.

"Reasonable, dude."

Huh?

"She didn't see me get in the podium, Bird Bones. In her world, I was there, in the classroom, and then, all of a sudden, I disappeared. If you ask me, it's good to know our teacher cares enough about her students to get upset when they vanish into thin air."

I'm not saying I'm totally convinced by his argument. But I will say this: Ms. Gribbs was so happy to see Stu sitting in his desk again that she didn't even punish him. Ms. Gribbs's student had been lost, but now he was found.

She called the principal back and told him, "Never mind, the student has re-materialized." (I can only imagine how confusing these two phone calls must have been for Principal Davis.)

Stu Negotiates with Terrorists

There were exactly thirty-nine desks in Ms. Gribbs's class, and—including Ms. Gribbs—there were exactly thirty-nine bodies. It was a perfect fit. Or it would have been, if Ms. Gribbs wasn't—to use the technical term—straight bonkers. More specifically, we would have had enough desks for everyone if it wasn't for Ms. Gribbs's box of markers. Her love for that thing knew no bounds. She loved her box of markers so much that she gave it a name: Janice.

I'm not kidding.

And that's not all. She loved that box of markers so much that she gave it a desk.

I'm serious.

Justin Richards spent the year sitting on the floor so "Janice" could "sit" on a desk. Not just any desk, either: Janice sat on the desk directly across the room from Ms. Gribbs, so she could always keep an eye on "her."

In Ms. Gribbs's defense, she felt bad enough about this that she sometimes gave Justin a mini candy bar from the stash in her office. Honestly, I think Justin might have told you it was a fair trade. The only time he didn't look miserable sitting there was when he was devouring another candy bar. I don't know what it is about candy at school, but it tastes way better than candy anywhere else.

As for Janice, none of us knew why she was so important to Ms. Gribbs. There were theories, though. The most popular one was that the marker box had been given to her by a favorite student named Janice. Something tragic had happened to her. According to Josh Noren, who had talked with his older brother, who had talked with a senior at the high school, the real Janice had gone missing one day and never came back.

Maybe that's exactly what happened. It would sort of explain Ms. Gribbs's freak-out when Stu "disappeared."

Then again, maybe Ms. Gribbs was—to use the psychiatric term—a total whack job.

Personally, I thought she might be using the markers to do her makeup in the morning. The various colors on her face always had a smeared-on quality. The red on her thin lips looked more like a Kool Aid stain than regular lipstick. Maybe, when she was coloring in some eye shadow, the ink sank into her skull and then her brain.

Of course, that would mean she actually opened the box and used the markers inside—something that was apparently a bad idea. At the beginning of the year, Melissa Crabtree had picked up Janice while working on a poster board presentation and learned quickly enough she'd made a grave mistake. "CAREFUL!" Ms. Gribbs had shrieked as Melissa flipped open a latch. She kept on shrieking ("Be gentle! Take it easy!") as Melissa opened the next latch and lifted the lid. It was like the box was booby-trapped. One false move and we all went kablewey. It didn't take Melissa long to decide that the markers weren't worth the anxiety.

Since then, nobody had tried to use a single marker.

No one . . . except Stu.

He took the whole box.

Ms. Gribbs was in her office looking for something when Stu stood up from his desk and took a few long strides across the room. When he got to Janice's desk, he stopped. He scratched his chin as though deep in thought. There was something about Stu's movements that always seemed theatrical. I think it was because his arms and legs were so long. When he took a step, it was so much longer than anyone else's that it seemed to happen in slow motion.

This was an illusion, of course. Stu's long strides actually made him faster than most of us because he covered so much ground in so few steps.

The illusion was in full effect as he bent at the waist and reached for the marker box. Any second now, Ms. Gribbs would return to the room, but it didn't seem like it was taking Stu seconds to pick up the box. It felt more like minutes.

Hours, even.

Stu, of course, was fully aware of this illusion, and milked it as much as possible. Have you ever seen a silent movie? Or a mime? If so, you probably understand the dramatic possibilities of exaggerated movement.

Stu held up the box for all of us to see. He kept it up there, way up high above his head, as he took a few more long strides toward his desk.

Whatever he was planning to do, he needed to hurry: Ms. Gribbs never left the room for long.

But Stu didn't hurry, or at least he didn't appear to. He sat in his desk and lowered the box of markers. He winced as he set the box down, as though the sound of it landing on the desktop would give him away. With his thumbs, he flipped open the latches. He winced again as he slowly, slowly pried open the box. Stu took out a blue marker and held it up for our benefit. The marker was in his right hand, his strong hand, but he moved it to his left. (He later told me he had done this to disguise his handwriting.) He had a notebook on the table, already opened, and he began to write.

When he finished writing, he held the note up for us to see.

We took Janice hostage, the message read. Sincerely, The class Down the Hall

As we read the message, and without even looking, Stu put the blue marker back inside, closed the box, and reached for his backpack, which was lying next to his desk. He unzipped the backpack, put the marker box inside, and zipped it back up.

All of this happened at the very moment Ms. Gribbs's office door was opening.

"Dude, Ms. G," Stu said when she emerged. "They took your markers."

"Wha—what are you talking about?" she stuttered. She whipped her head around and found Janice's empty desk.

"We tried to stop them," Stu said, "but they came too quickly. They must have been training for weeks."

"For the love of all that is decent, who's THEY?" Ms. Gribbs shrieked.

"I don't know," Stu said. "They were wearing masks. But they left this."

He handed her the message he'd just written.

When Ms. Gribbs finished reading the message, she bolted for the door. Stu took one long sideways step and cut her off. He explained that it wasn't a good idea for her try to get the box back because she was too emotionally invested in the outcome. I remember him using that phrase, "emotionally invested." Actually, I'm pretty sure I remember the whole conversation, but I'm not going to include it here, because if I did, you probably wouldn't believe me. You'd think I was making it up. You'd think, *Okay, Ms. Gribbs* might *have been crazy, but she couldn't have possibly been this dumb.* How could a grown woman possibly believe her *markers* had been *ransomed* by the kids across the hall? It's a fair question—but only because you didn't know Ms. Gribbs, and more important, because you didn't know Stu. When Stu was around, you started to expect the impossible. He had a way of explaining crazy, ridiculous things so they sounded totally logical.

That's how he convinced Ms. Gribbs to let him be the negotiator. He talked about psychology and strategy and tactics. He explained that taller people always had the advantage in a conversation. "Why do you think talk show hosts sit higher than their guests?" he asked Ms. Gribbs.

And by the time he was finished talking, Ms. Gribbs practically begged him to go find the right classroom and use his height to gain a tactical edge.

Stu said he would do his best. Then he strapped on his backpack like it was part of his negotiator outfit and left the room. He later told me that what he did next was walk to his locker, rip out another sheet of paper from another notebook, write a new message with his left hand, put the marker box into his locker, and head back to our classroom.

Of course, Ms. Gribbs didn't know any of this. She spent those minutes eyeing the door and biting her nails.

Stu returned with a somber face. "They gave me their terms," he said. He cleared his throat and read the message he'd just written. "Give us all your candy or say good-bye to Janice."

Stu looked up from the message. "Usually I don't think negotiating with terrorists is a good policy," he said, "but in this case—"

He didn't have a chance to finish his sentence because Ms. Gribbs was already hustling for her office. She emerged a few seconds later with three full bags of mini candy bars.

"Get her back, Stu," she said. "Please, please get her back."

"I'll do my best, Ms. G," he said. He reached behind his head, unzipped his backpack, and shoved the bags of candy inside.

A few tense minutes later, he returned, his backpack still bulging.

He didn't say anything, just got on a knee, reached behind his shoulder blades with both arms, and removed the marker box as though he was unsheathing a sword from a back scabbard. He ducked his head and extended the marker box to Ms. Gribbs.

Ms. Gribbs took the box as though a great treasure had been returned to her by a valiant knight.

The rest of the class was now looking directly at the backpack. It was *still* bulging, and there was one final note attached to it.

Anyone want some candy? it said. Rendezvous at my locker.

Ms. Gribbs carried Janice—carefully, tenderly—into her office, put "her" in the still-open bottom drawer, closed the drawer, and locked it.

We never saw the marker box again.

After class, everyone who knew the definition of *rendezvous* met Stu at his locker and got a king-size candy bar's worth of mini candy bars.

The next day, Stu suggested that Justin Richards could sit in the now-empty desk. As she always did, Ms. Gribbs agreed with him.

"I'll tell you what, Bird Bones," Stu said to me at lunch. "I must be the only negotiator in history to get everyone involved everything they wanted."

How I Got the Name "Bird Bones"

Think of this book as a comic book. If you've ever read a comic book, you know they often feature secondary stories about secondary action heroes. Sometimes, years later, these secondary action heroes get their own comic books.

This is not one of those times.

Truthfully, I don't really like to talk about myself. As a general rule, I don't think you'll find me as interesting as Stu. I definitely don't.

It seems to me that some of you, though, might be interested in why Stu started calling me "Bird Bones."

It happened on the first day of eighth grade, at football practice.

But before I talk about that, I need to rewind a bit more to earlier that day in science class.

That was when our teacher, Mr. Ogren, held up a bird's skeleton. It was glued to a piece of construction paper so that it provided a two-dimensional outline of the bird's natural shape. Mr. Ogren told us bird skeletons were different than human skeletons.

"For instance," he said, "birds have beaks instead of noses and mouths." He actually paused to let this observation sink in. "If you look closely," he continued, "you will also notice they have wings rather than arms." After another long pause, he concluded, "That's why they can fly and we can't."

I'm pretty sure he actually thought he was telling us stuff we didn't already know.

I was just about to tune him out entirely when he finally did say something I didn't know.

"Wings," he said, "aren't the only reason birds can fly."

Mr. Ogren ripped one of the bones off the bird skeleton, taking a strip of the construction paper with it. He pinched the bone between his fingers and snapped it in half. Then he turned the two pieces of bone in our direction. "Unlike our bones, most bird bones are hollow," he said. "This makes them appear lightweight. It's also what makes flight possible."

It was actually a pretty cool demonstration.

Or that's what I thought, anyway, until I went to football practice after school.

Since it was the first day of practice, we were all lined up in the gym to get weighed in. One by one we stepped on a scale to determine which team we would play for. If a kid weighed more than 125 pounds, he played on the heavyweight squad. If he weighed less than 125 pounds, he played on the lightweight squad. The goal was safety, I think, and that was fine by me.

Put simply, I was pretty puny back then. Okay, *really* puny. Puny enough that this was the first year my parents had allowed me to play football. Puny enough that I had no interest in getting trampled by boys my age who had already received huge doses of that steroid called puberty.

The only reason I was even playing tackle football was so my teammates would let me play touch football during recess. The school I went to was called Babbling Brook, and it was one of the last combined elementary and middle schools in the Midwest. Every day after lunch, some of the seventh and eighth grade boys would play a huge game of touch football in the field next to the playground. If you didn't get asked to play, your options were limited. You could go on the playground with the younger kids, or . . .

Come to think of it, that was pretty much it.

Anyway, I figured if I was on the real team, I'd get to be on one of the recess teams too.

And unlike other sports, the football team didn't cut anyone. All you had to do to be on the team was sign up.

Or that's what I thought . . . until I stepped on the scale.

"I'm sorry, Hueller," the coach said. "It says here you only weigh 79 pounds."

I didn't know what to say. Was it really necessary for him to announce my weight out loud for everyone to hear? Did he think I was hoping to be on the heavyweight squad? I just got in line because everyone else did.

"The minimum weight to play football in eighth grade is 85 pounds," he said.

I was stunned. Literally. I didn't move from the scale.

"You want me to try again?" he asked. "Maybe I messed up. You look to me like you weigh at least 86, 87 pounds."

I think he was trying to be fair—even compassionate. But he was just making it worse. I could feel all my classmates watching me, amused.

"Let's see here . . ." he said, fiddling with the scale. He turned back to me. "I'm sorry, son," he said again. "This scale . . . it doesn't lie. There's nothing I can do."

I was on my way back across the gym when I heard him say, "I could have sworn you weighed more than 79 measly pounds."

Chad Logan, the biggest bully in our grade, but also someone with a knack for giving great insulting nicknames, said, "Patrick must have bird bones!" When everyone laughed, he knew he was on to something. "Isn't that right, Bird Bones? Do you have bird bones, Bird Bones?"

I couldn't sleep that night, because I knew what had just happened. Being cut from a team that didn't cut anyone was bad enough. But getting nicknamed by Chad Logan? His nicknames had staying power. What if *Bird Bones* followed me all the way through high school?

The only chance I had, I decided, was to keep quiet about it. Maybe the nickname wasn't as memorable to everyone else as it was to me.

Fat chance.

Chad Logan was there to make sure they remembered. "Everyone," he said as soon as I arrived at school, "Bird Bones is here! Give Bird Bones a round of applause!"

Whether everyone clapped or not, I couldn't tell. My ears were pounding too loud from shame.

Chad kept at it throughout the morning.

By the time I sat down with Stu at lunch, I thought my life as a normal, average, regularly named kid was over.

Stu agreed with me.

But unlike me, he thought it was a great thing.

"Bird Bones," he said aloud. "I can't believe it. Bird Bones! That's like the coolest nickname I've ever heard, dude!"

"What are you talking about?" I asked.

It was Italian dunker day at lunch. As far as I could tell, that was the only thing good about this day. I felt like I was eating my last good meal before my execution.

"What do you mean what am I talking about?" Stu asked. "You've basically been given a superhero's name. Bird Bones. It's like you can fly . . . or walk on snow without breaking the surface!"

I hadn't thought of it like that.

Stu dunked his Italian dunker in red sauce. "Cheers are in order," he said. "To the one and only Bird Bones."

We clinked our dunkers together in celebration.

That afternoon, a teacher took attendance. When she got to my name, I said, "Call me Bird Bones."

She didn't take me up on my offer, and neither did the rest of my classmates. Now that I had embraced it, no one seemed as interested in saying it. Chad Logan still broke the name out from time to time, but only because he hadn't been able to come up with another one.

The only person who called me Bird Bones all the time was Stu. And I felt like a superhero every time he said it.

Stu Goes Undercover

Sometime that fall, a boys-only assembly was called. We all went to the auditorium and watched Mr. Baker, the assistant principal, stomp across the stage.

Mr. Baker was a huge, angry, bear of a man. He must have weighed close to four hundred pounds. When he spoke into the microphone, it sounded more like a growl.

"One of you, or maybe many of you, has been scratching images on the bathroom stall doors," he growled.

Of course, I knew exactly what he was referring to. Everyone did. I'm not going to go into details, but let's just say the images were impossible to miss.

Mr. Baker had other ways of describing them.

"They are foul, filthy, and unfathomably offensive," he growled. "Whoever did this . . . whoever made these horrifying, repulsive, disgusting images . . ."

Mr. Baker couldn't finish his sentence.

He was too busy crying.

This monstrous man was all of a sudden bawling monstrous tears.

It was shocking.

I was used to seeing his sweat drip to the floor—but his tears?

I think that's why some of the boys in the auditorium laughed at him. Have you ever heard of people laughing at funerals? It actually happens quite often. And it's not because the person laughing thinks there's anything funny about death. Just the opposite. The laughter is a way to release anxiety. Watching a terrifying man like Mr. Baker cry was a different sort of terrifying, and I think some of the boys in the auditorium laughed because they didn't know what else to do.

In any case, laughing at Mr. Baker in that moment was a bad idea.

"You think this is funny?" he growled, his tears evaporating on his sizzling hot jowls. "Stall doors are a privilege, gentleman—a privilege you clearly do not take seriously. They will be returned to you when I'm convinced they are no longer a laughing matter."

True to his word, Mr. Baker had all the stall doors in the boys' bathrooms removed.

I don't know how you feel about sitting on a toilet with your pants down while a huge line of others stares right at you—but me? I didn't like it. In fact, I couldn't think of many things that would be worse.

"You better not have had anything to do with those images," I told Stu at lunch.

Stu winced at the accusation.

"I'm hurt, Bird Bones," he said. "Do you really think that's my style? Mr. Baker was right. Those images were disgusting, dude."

I knew right away he was telling the truth. Stu might have wanted to be legendary, but there were limits to what he would do, and vandalism was definitely one of them.

"Sorry," I told him. "So do you think Mr. Baker was right to take the stall doors?"

"No way, dude. Punishing innocent people is never right."

Now *this* sounded like the Stu I knew. He was never one to tolerate injustice.

"So what are you going to do?" I asked him.

My brain started whirring with top-secret stealth missions to locate the stall doors and return them to their rightful stalls.

"Me?" Stu said. He chugged his milk and picked up his tray. "I'm going to join the swim team, dude."

Like Mr. Baker, Stu was true to his word. That very day he started practicing with the swim team. I knew because of the way he smelled of chlorine. And because of the brand-new, bright-blue swim bag he started using as a backpack.

And because he shaved his legs.

"It makes me more aerodynamic, dude," he explained to me before English class. "Lots of swimmers do it."

"Fine," I said. "But why are you wearing shorts to school? It's getting cold outside."

"To show off my legs," he said.

His voice was matter-of-fact, as though I'd asked a stupid question and he'd given me the obvious answer. But the answer didn't seem obvious to me at all. Besides the fact that it was freezing outside, shaved legs weren't exactly something to brag about. Don't get me wrong— it made total sense that a swimmer would shave his legs; male or female, athletes need to do what they need to do. But Stu was the first guy I'd ever seen who was so proud of his hairless legs that he wanted to flaunt them in public.

Besides, when he rolled up his sleeves one day before dipping a dunker in red sauce, I noticed something strange.

"That's . . . arm hair," I said.

"True, Bird Bones," Stu said. "And this"—he pointed to his face—"is my nose. Seriously, dude, are you feeling all right?"

"No, I mean, why do you have arm hair?"

When Stu started explaining puberty to me, I interrupted. "That's not what I'm asking, Stu. I'm asking why you didn't shave your arm hair when you did shave your leg hair."

Stu took a big gulp from his milk carton. He swirled the milk around his mouth, then gurgled it.

"Quit stalling," I said.

He swallowed. Then he lifted his arms into the air and said, "You caught me, dude."

"Caught you doing what?"

"Come to the meet tonight, Bird Bones, and all your questions will be answered."

Stu said I was going to get answers at the swim meet, but at first all I got were more questions.

It wasn't just his arms he hadn't shaved. Stu had tufts of hair on his chest, his stomach, and under his armpits.

Unlike all the other swimmers, he didn't have a swim cap or even goggles.

And while the others were wearing speedos, Stu had on a giant, baggy pair of swim trunks.

Not exactly aerodynamic attire.

It was hard to imagine someone looking less like a swimmer, which made sense, once he got into the water. When it was his turn to race, he got up on the starting block. Like the other swimmers in his heat, he waited for the horn to go off. When it did, everyone dove into the water headfirst.

Everyone, that is, except for Stu. He went in feet first and with a huge splash. A cannon ball would have been more elegant. Then he began thrashing away at the water as though his life depended on it.

Actually, I'm pretty sure it did. There were several times I thought Stu might drown right in front of me.

By the time he got to the other end of the pool, the others were heading back the other way. Stu had expended all his energy getting to this end of the pool; how was he going to get back to the other end?

The answer was that he wasn't.

Instead of touching the wall and turning around, Stu lifted a giant leg and stepped right out of the pool. Then he headed for the locker room. Before he got there, he looked into the stands, locked eyes with me, and waved his arm just enough to let me know I was supposed to follow him.

I did.

I couldn't get to the pool from the bleachers, so I walked by the concession area and then the ticketing booth. When I finally entered the boys' locker room from the other side, I was surprised to find it totally empty. I spent some time looking for Stu, but honestly, there weren't too many places to look. The showers were empty. The locker area was empty. And the stalls, still doorless, were empty.

It wasn't until I decided to give up that I noticed all the puddles.

Now, puddles in a swimming locker might not sound surprising. But these puddles didn't just lead in and out of the shower area. They also led to the opposite the door—the door I'd used only minutes before.

On a hunch, I followed these puddles—out the door and then . . . into the *girls'* locker room.

Don't worry. I didn't go into the girls' locker room. Not at first.

"Stu?" I said through the door. I meant to shout it but I was too embarrassed and ended up saying it almost under my breath.

"What took you so long, dude?" Stu's voice boomed.

For better or worse, my curiosity got the best of me.

"You shouldn't be in here," I said as I passed through the locker area.

"Trust me, Bird Bones," Stu said. "You fit in way less than I do."

I followed his voice into the bathroom area.

That's when I saw that we weren't alone. There was a girl in one of the stalls.

Well, not a girl—a woman.

I could only see her high heels and some of her legs. On the ground, next to the base of the toilet, was a brand-new, bright-blue swimming bag.

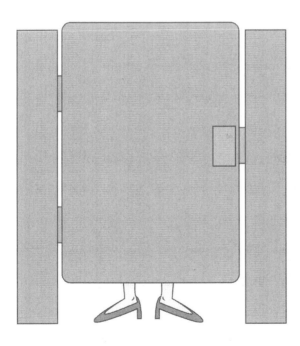

It was only then that it dawned on me how big the woman's feet were.

"Stu? I said through the stall door. "Is that you?"

The door swung open.

"C'mon in, dude," he said.

There he was, sitting on a closed toilet (with his swim trunks still on!).

"What . . . ?" I stammered. "What are you doing here?"

He didn't answer, and he didn't need to. I was putting it together just fine on my own.

"Wait," I said, "so you're saying you joined the swim team, shaved your legs, bought a brand-new swim bag—"

Here Stu interrupted me: "Don't forget women's shoes, Bird Bones. I had to buy those too. It's not easy to find size fifteen high heels."

"And you did all this to avoid going to the bathroom in a stall without a door?"

"Exactly, dude."

I thought about this for a moment.

Yeah—it made total sense to me.

Stu Becomes an Art Thief

Ms. Delfry was my middle school art teacher. But she didn't look like any art teacher I had ever seen.

Rather than paint- and clay-spattered jeans and shirts, Ms. Delfry wore spotless business outfits.

Rather than comfortable shoes, she wore high heels.

As far as I could tell, she found most of the art supplies in the room either icky or dangerous and tried to keep away from them as much as possible.

Especially after she got braces.

Why she got them, none of us were sure. As far as we could tell, her teeth had looked perfectly fine.

Then again, Ms. Delfry wasn't aiming for perfectly fine. To use her words, she was aiming for "permanence in an impermanent world."

She always talked like that.

On this particular day, she said, "Have you noticed my latest experiential artistic installation?" She waved her arm toward a side table with a giant fruit basket on it.

"You mean the fruit basket?" someone finally said.

"This is no mere produce package," Ms. Delfry said, moving to the table. She pointed to the fruit. "Who can tell me what this is?" she asked.

Was this a trick question?

"Fruit?" one kid finally said.

"Yes," Ms. Delfry said through her braces, "but what kind of fruit is it?"

Finally, we felt like we were on solid ground.

"Bananas," one kid said.

"Oranges," said another.

"Grapes!"

Ms. Delfry let kids keep naming fruits in the basket until she couldn't take it any longer. "The answer I was looking for," she said, "was *fake*." She paused to let that sink in. "This is all fake fruit," she repeated, then paused again for dramatic effect. "Or is it?" she asked.

After another pause—not for dramatic effect but because we were all confused—someone said, "No?"

"Exactly," Ms. Delfry said. "Indeed, most of this fruit is fake. But amongst these impostors resides the authentic article—one solitary object that is more than plastic and paint. At the moment, it's impossible to find the real fruit. But you just wait—an hour, a day, two days—soon enough, the real fruit will begin to ripen and then to rot. You see, this installation is no mere fruit basket," Ms. Delfry continued, enunciating her words carefully through her braces. "On the contrary, it is a reminder to all of us that life, real life, is decay, decrepitude, deterioration. Life, children, is death. And this fruit basket satirically symbolizes—"

She never got to finish her sentence, because right then Stu lurched out of his desk, launched himself across the room, and grabbed a peach from the middle of the basket. The other fruit went tumbling to the ground as Stu took a giant bite.

He'd picked correctly: orange juice dribbled down the corners of his mouth and dripped off his chin.

"Shame to waste perfectly good fruit, eh Ms. D?" he said.

Then he took another chomp of the peach.

This wasn't just a one-time thing.

The first time it happened, Ms. Delfry yelled at Stu and made him stay after class. The next day, we found the fruit basket once again on the table. The fake fruit had been carefully piled; the real peach had been carefully placed in the exact same place as before.

This time, Stu waited for Ms. Delfry to go back to her desk before pouncing.

Plastic produce plummeted to the floor as Stu took a bite from the still-perfect peach.

Ms. Delfry couldn't believe her eyes. "What . . . what are you doing?" she gasped.

I had the same question. Stu was always up to something, and often that something made teachers' lives more difficult. But it wasn't like him to damage other people's property. In fact, Stu seemed to take pride in the fact that he never hurt anyone or anything.

All Stu would say—to Ms. Delfry and to me—was "Fruit is meant to be eaten."

Apparently, for him, it was as simple as that.

Or maybe not.

The more I think about it, the more I think Stu had deeper reasons for his actions. I'm pretty sure he was offended by Ms. Delfry's "art installation," that eating the fruit was his way of taking a stand against Ms. Delfry and her fruit basket. He wanted—needed?—Ms. Delfry and the rest of us to know she was wrong. Fruit didn't represent decay and death. It represented . . .

Food?

Energy?

Life?

Your guess is as good as mine.

Over the next several days, Ms. Delfry tried everything she could think of to stop Stu from eating the fruit.

She moved the basket to harder-to-reach places. The problem, of course, was that Stu was almost seven feet tall, so something that was hard to reach for Ms. Delfry was a cinch for him.

When moving the basket didn't work, she changed the fruit. Rather than always having the one real fruit be a peach, she mixed it up. Sometimes it would be an apple, or a banana, or an orange.

This didn't work, either.

I don't know how Stu did it—but he always picked the right fruit.

Finally, Ms. Delfry got so desperate that she found a way to make us stay in our desks. "Today is the day," she announced, "for the big exam I've been telling you about. I hope you're prepared." Immediately, kids' hands shot up in the air. We'd never heard of this exam, let alone prepared for it. Since when did middle school art classes give exams? Ms. Delfry didn't call on anyone, though. She was too busy handing out the exam.

"I'm sorry, students," she said. "But the time for questions is over. If you have questions, you should have asked them before the day of the test."

Looking back, I realize she made up the exam so she could bring in more adult supervision. Their job, she told us, was to make sure no one cheated. There was to be no looking at each other's work, and no getting up until the end of the period. We were not even going to be granted a bathroom or water break.

The whole thing was pretty crazy. All of this just to prevent a student from eating a piece of fruit? Amanda Billows, the biggest perfectionist in our grade, was literally sobbing in her desk. That's how overwhelmed she was by this pop exam.

Then again, it was pretty genius too. Ms. Delfry had waited until a Friday to have the exam, which meant all she needed to do was keep Stu away from the fruit for one day. After that, it would have an entire weekend to rot.

Watching Stu try to get to the fruit basket that day was like watching a heist movie. You know the movies I'm talking about? The ones where the thief is stealing a priceless painting from a museum or a bunch of gold bars from a vault in Vegas? Where he or she has to contort his or her body around lasers while staying out of sight of a roving camera?

Okay, so there weren't lasers in Ms. Delfry's room. Or cameras. But just getting out of his desk was an impressive feat. He waited for all four sets of adult eyes to briefly turn away from him, then he straightened his long legs and slid right off his seat like a piece of paper.

He army crawled his way through the rest of our desks. Somehow he always seemed to know where every adult eye was at all times.

Slowly, stealthily, he slithered his way to Ms. Delfry's desk.

That's where she had finally decided to keep the fruit basket. Right in front of her, where she never had to lose sight of it.

When Stu made it to the side of her desk, he disappeared from view.

How he did what he did next I really don't know.

If you weren't watching as closely as I was, you might have missed it completely.

Ms. Delfry did.

Stu must have been a great Jenga player, because at lightning-quick speed I saw his big hand reach around to the front of the fruit bowl and remove a pear *without toppling the rest of the fruit.* I think the basket wobbled a bit, but then again, maybe not: this had all happened right in front of Ms. Delfry's face, and she hadn't noticed a thing.

Nor did she notice Stu as he made his way back to his desk on all fours.

No, come to think of it, the basket *must* have wobbled: it's the only explanation for how the fruit finally teetered and collapsed all over Ms. Delfry. From the wreckage, Ms. Delfry turned to Stu's desk. There he was, sitting quietly, diligently working on his exam.

While munching on the pear.

Ms. Delfry was so angry she actually suspended Stu. She must have reported him for cheating on the exam, or at least for getting out of his desk without permission during an exam. But besides the pear in his hand, what was her proof? None of the adults had seen Stu leave his desk.

In any case, we all knew the real reason: Stu was the first and only kid to get suspended for eating fruit.

The suspension lasted for two weeks.

By the time Stu got back, Ms. Delfry's fruit basket looked the way she wanted it to. A bunch of perfect-looking fake fruit and one rotten, moldy peach. As a class, we had watched the fruit go dark, then white with furry mold. Flies had flocked, and Ms. Delfry had won her strange contest with Stu.

Or that's how it seemed . . . until Stu returned.

And slipped out of his desk.

And crawled to the front of the room.

And grabbed the rotten, moldy, furry peach.

And took a giant bite.

"Fruit is made to be eaten," he said again, his mouth full.

The juice dribbling out of the corners of his mouth may have been brown, but his smile was so big that it sure looked to me as though it was Stu who had bested Ms. Delfry, and not the other way around.

Stu's Head Falls Off

One day, at the beginning of class, Stu's head fell off. Or at least that's what Stu wanted everyone to think. He'd explained his plan to me at lunch.

"Check it out, Bird Bones," he'd said. He took the pastrami out of his pastrami sandwich and placed it on top of his head. Then he tucked his head inside his shirt.

"Does it look like I've been decapitated, dude?"

"What does decapitated mean?" I asked.

"Like my head fell off," he said through his shirt.

I looked at him closer. The shape of his nose was clearly visible through his shirt. Some of his hair sprouted above the shirt collar.

"It looks more like you have pastrami on your head," I said.

"Dude," he said through his shirt, "that's not pastrami. It's the gory remains of my neck after my head fell off."

"Weird," I said. "It looks like pastrami."

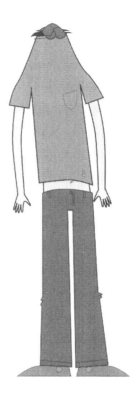

"That's only because you saw me put it there, Bird Bones. If you hadn't, you'd definitely think it was the gory remains of my neck after my head fell off."

"Whatever you say, Stu."

"Besides," Stu added, still talking through his shirt, "when I get decapitated next period, I'm going to yell about how much pain I'm in. It'll be really dramatic."

"How are you going to yell if you don't have a head?" I pointed out. I thought it was a good point, but Stu was unimpressed.

"The same way movies set in space have loud, fiery explosions," he said through his shirt.

"Huh?"

"In real life, Bird Bones, explosions in space wouldn't make a sound," he said.

"They wouldn't?"

"To have a boom you need oxygen," Stu said. "There's no oxygen in space."

"Good point," I said.

"No it's not, dude."

"It's not?"

"No, it's not. Look, Bird Bones, the reason space-ships explode in fiery blazes isn't because people think that's what would really happen. It's because a silent, un-fiery explosion is boring." He pulled his head through his collar and took the pastrami off his head. "Same goes for heads falling off," he said, putting the pastrami in his pants pocket. "A decapitation without gore and without screaming is no fun at all."

And if that's what Stu was going for—entertain-ment—he definitely succeeded.

Our next class after lunch was called Personal Family Life Science, aka PFLS. So far that semester, we'd learned how to do a load of laundry, how to make brownies, and how to treat an egg like it was our baby. At the moment, we were all sewing boxers.

The rest of us were in front of our sewing machines when Stu arrived.

As promised, he made his arrival as dramatic as possible.

Stu was so tall that he had to duck to make it through doors. On this day, he simply "forgot" to duck. There was a large banging sound that was supposed to represent his head hitting the doorframe but was actually Stu kicking the door as hard as he could.

Apparently, we were supposed to believe he had hit his head so hard that it tore completely off his body, because Stu came stumbling in with only (to use his words) "the gory remains of his neck." Of course, it didn't actually look anything at all like gore; what it looked like was pastrami and a little bit of hair. His shirt was pulled up so high that we could see his hairy bellybutton.

"Ow, dudes!" Stu bellowed through his shirt. "Look! My head—it's totally gone! Oh, the agony! The horror! How am I supposed to go through life without a head?"

If all he wanted to do was amuse people, it worked. Everyone shook their heads and laughed.

Everyone, anyway, except for our teacher, Ms. Pederson.

She screamed.

In pain.

And unlike Stu, her pain was real.

So was her gore.

Okay, maybe gore is an overstatement.

But there really was blood. Apparently, Ms. Pederson had been so startled by Stu's antics that she'd managed to sew two of her fingers together.

Why she had been so startled, I'm truly not sure. Was it the banging on the doorframe? It was hard to believe it was Stu's ridiculous bellowing. It was even harder to believe it was "the gory remains of his neck." Then again, I suppose it doesn't take much to hurt yourself at a sewing machine. Just one twitch can do it.

In her defense, Ms. Pederson didn't overdo the pain. She didn't roll on the floor. She didn't howl. There was one quick scream—a yelp is more like it—and then she sat there wincing and staring at her bloody fingers.

It was Stu who overdid it. He pulled his shirt down, saw what had happened to our teacher, and galloped across the room. Before she knew what was going on, Stu had scooped her up and carried her out of the classroom. It was Stu who took her to the front office, and it was Stu who called 911. He even rode in the ambulance with her.

According to Ms. Pederson the next day, Stu had been very gallant. The medics had needed to assure him several times that she would be just fine.

When Stu finally calmed down, a medic said, "Can I ask you a question?"

"Sure, dude," Stu said.

"Why do you have pastrami on your head?"

How I Fell in Love

By the winter of eighth grade, I was pretty sure I was in love with a girl named Clara Berns. I was also pretty sure she didn't know I existed. We had definitely never spoken. In fact, in the three months I'd known *she* existed, I'd only heard her say a handful of words. She never talked in class, or in the halls, or at lunch. Instead, she read. Everywhere. She'd read in class until a teacher had to tell her to put the book down. She'd read as she walked down the hall. She'd read as she got her tray and then her food in the lunch line. Honestly, it was weird. Who loved reading books that much?

But it was also why I was pretty sure I was in love with her. Don't get me wrong. I wasn't pretty sure I was in love with her because she read a lot. I was pretty sure I was in love with her because she didn't seem to care she was being weird. By choosing books over people, she was committing social suicide. Chad Logan picked on her all the time. He even came up with a mean nickname for her: Clarasil. (As I mentioned earlier, Chad had a knack for mean nicknames. He called Justin Richards, for instance, Just Rich—which fit Justin perfectly. Not only did Justin have to sit on the floor in Ms. Gribbs's class, but he also pretty much dismissed or outright ignored wherever he went. No one disliked him; they just didn't seem to care about him one way or the other. He had a tendency to wander around day-dreaming, which made him both harmless and weird. When Chad saw him in the hallway, he'd shrug his shoulders and say, "Look everyone—it's Just Rich" or "Nothing to see here. It's Just Rich." In other words, Chad was saying, it wasn't anyone important—just Rich.)

In Clara's case, I think he was making fun of her for having some acne on her face. Clearasil is a zit cream, and since it sounded kind of like her name, the nickname made good bully sense. Like any good bully nickname, it should have hurt her feelings. But as far as I could tell, it didn't. She just ignored him and kept reading.

Take, for example, this one time during recess. As usual, I was sitting on the edge of the playground, pretending to stare off into space. There was nothing better to do: playing on the playground was for the younger kids. And as I said before, I'd never been invited to play football with the rest of the eighth grade guys. Besides, I wasn't actually staring off into space. I was trying to find Stu. The guy was amazing: we'd eat lunch together every day; we'd put our trays away together; we'd even walk to recess together. Then he'd say, "See you later, Bird Bones," and within a few minutes, no matter how hard I tried to keep an eye on him, I would completely lose sight of him. He was almost seven feet tall, but he was nowhere to be found.

At the beginning of the year, I went around looking for him, but that got old quick. By that winter I had all but given up. Still, I couldn't help glancing around the playground every few minutes, just in case I caught a glance of my mysterious friend. When I wasn't looking for Stu, I was looking at Clara Berns. Not for long, though. I did my best not to stare. But honestly, it was hard for me to keep my eyes off her.

Like me, she could always be found in the same place. In her case, that place was the tire swing. I'm not sure why she chose to sit there. It definitely wasn't to swing. She just sat there, straddling the tire, reading yet another book. When little kids would come up and ask if they could take a turn on the tire, Clara wouldn't even look up:

"I'm sorry," she'd tell them. "This tire swing will be occupied for the remainder of recess." Then she went back to her book, as though the kid wasn't still standing there. Except she did know. I was sure of it. Because unlike everyone else, I wasn't looking at her face or the book it was planted in. I was looking at her calves. They were magnificent. They were the biggest, strongest, best calves I'd ever seen. Except I hadn't seen them—not really. For some reason, Clara made a point of covering them up.

It was the beginning of winter now, so the fact that she wore long pants made sense. But what didn't make sense was that she even wore long pants during PE even though our gymnasium was basically like a sauna. Another mystery: why didn't she ever try during PE? With calves like hers, I knew she must be really fast—but no matter how many times Mr. Fishly, our PE teacher, told her to put the book down and show a little effort, she never moved faster than a walk.

Was she ashamed of how muscular her calves were? Why would she be embarrassed about being super fast or jumping super high? The only time I got a glimpse of her wondrous calves was when she sat on that tire swing. She'd plant her feet firmly into the woodchips and her calf muscles would bulge, stretching the bottom of her pant legs. Do you think it's weird that I'm going on and on about calf muscles? That I'm using words like *magnificent* and *wondrous* to describe them? If so, I don't care. I'm not at all ashamed to admit I loved those calf muscles. I also loved that I was apparently the only one who knew about them. If Clara wanted to keep them hidden, that was fine by me; they could be our little secret. That's what I was thinking the day the football sailed over my head, bounced sideways on the woodchips, and came to rest a few inches from one of Clara's sneakers.

"Hey, Clarasil," Chad Logan yelled from the icy field. "A little help?"

As usual, Clara ignored him.

"Hey, Clarasil!" Chad yelled again. "I'm talking to you!" Still no response. Like all bullies, Chad didn't like to be ignored. I think he took it as a sign of disrespect, as though his authority was being undermined. Usually, he would have made someone else go get the football. But getting ignored completely, in front of all the other football players and all the other kids he liked to intimidate, was too much. He decided to take matters into his own hands.

"Clarasil!" he yelled once more, only this time he was already on the move. "Yo, earth to Clarasil!" It didn't take him long to get to the playground and pick up the football. By then, he was piping-hot mad. "Hey! CLARASIL! Are you deaf?"

"I'm sorry," Clara said, her eyes still on her book. "This tire swing will be occupied for the remainder of recess."

It was one of the funniest things I'd ever seen— not to mention one of the scariest. Here was the biggest bully in our grade, standing right next to Clara, glaring down at her, and Clara spoke to him as though he was just a little kid wanting a turn on the tire. Chad started to tell her he wasn't there to ride a stupid tire swing— but he stopped himself.

"You know what?" he said, chucking the football over his shoulder. "Now that you mention it, I would like to go for a spin on this thing."

He grabbed one of the chains. "I'm sorry," Clara repeated. "This tire swing will be occupied for the remainder of recess." She still hadn't looked away from her book.

"I'm not asking," Chad said. "I'm telling." He pulled on the chain.

I think he thought it would only take one pull to send her tumbling out of the tire. But he was wrong. He tried again. And again. And again. Everyone else was probably trying to figure out how this was possible. But not me. Clara's calves were bigger than ever. They were straining to keep her sneakers planted in the wood-chips. Chad kept pulling, but neither the tire nor Clara budged an inch. Finally, Chad gave up and grabbed for Clara's shoulder. Unfortunately for him, science intervened. Chad had ground his feet all the way through the woodchips to the dirt below them. The woodchips had insulated this dirt from the winter cold, and it was therefore un-frozen and plenty slippery. What I'm trying to say is that rather than pull Clara off the tire, Chad slipped and fell.

Hard.

I half expected him to scramble back up and try again—but he didn't. At least on that day, during that recess, the bully had been defeated. When Chad finally did get up, he grabbed the football again and limped back to the field.

"I got the football," Chad announced weakly to the other players, as though everything had worked out as planned.

It was pretty pathetic. It was also really great.

Clara had never taken her eyes off her book.

"Did you see that, Bird Bones?"

I turned. Somehow, Stu had managed to materialize right next to me.

"Did *you* see that?" I asked.

He nodded enthusiastically.

"I'm pretty sure I'm in love with her, dude," he told me.

I nodded. I was no longer just pretty sure I was in love with her.

I knew it.

But I didn't tell him that, because—like Clara and her glorious calves—I wasn't ready to give up my secret.

Stu Does a Magic Trick

Good morning, Bird Bones!" Stu said to me.

"Hey," I said. "Do you mind telling me why you invited me here?"

"Because," he said, "I wanted to officially announce my decision to become a magician."

"Oh."

"Check this out, dude." Stu took off both of the mittens he was wearing and dropped them on the icy sidewalk. He unzipped a side pocket on his huge, puffy, Minnesota Vikings winter jacket and removed a small, thin, square scarf. He made a fist with the other hand and began jamming the scarf into it with his thumb. We were next to the school's flag pole, and Stu pushed off it with a booted foot. It was supposed to look like he was trying to get leverage as he jammed the scarf deeper into his fist. Finally, when the scarf was completely covered by his fist, Stu stood up and opened his hand.

"Abracadabra," he said. The scarf had vanished.

"Cool," I said.

"That's all you have to say, dude? Cool?"

"What else do you want me to say? It's 6 o'clock in the morning."

"Don't you want to know how it works, Bird Bones?"

"Maybe later in the morning," I said. Stu told me anyway.

"It's a fake thumb, dude. See?"

Sure enough, when I looked closer I could clearly see he was wearing a plastic thumb. Stu pulled it off his real thumb and pulled out the scarf. He showed me in slow motion how he had jammed the scarf into the fake thumb with his real thumb, then worn the fake thumb when he opened his hands.

"Cool," I said again. "But you could have waited until lunch to show me that. Or at least until we were inside."

It was the first really cold day of the winter, and I didn't want to be out here any longer than I had to.

"That's not my only trick," Stu said. He cupped his bare hands and blew into them to keep them warm.

"Seriously, Stu," I said, my teeth chattering. "Do we really have to be outside or—" I didn't get a chance to finish my sentence. Without warning, Stu turned around and stuck his tongue on the flagpole.

Do you know what happens to people who stick their tongues on a *metal* flagpole? In the middle of winter? It freezes instantly to the pole. If you think this is just a myth, trust me, it's not. The year before, some stupid second grader had licked the same pole on a dare. Let's just say he won the dare but lost some of his tongue. Even after pouring warm water on it, bits of that tongue stayed on the pole for at least another week. It was hard to believe anyone at Babbling Brook would ever try something like that again. Then again, Stu was new to the school, so he hadn't actually witnessed the gruesome results.

"No, Stu!" I yelled. But of course it was too late. His tongue was already on the pole, which meant it had already frozen stiff. Except it hadn't. Stu leaned back and his tongue came with him. He cupped his hands and blew on them again.

"Abracadabra," Stu said again. He opened his mouth wide to show me his tongue was still intact.

"How . . . how'd you do that?" I asked.

"Easy, Bird Bones," he said. "A fake tongue." He opened one of his hands and, sure enough, there was a rubber tongue.

"Where'd you get that?" I asked.

"Cut it out of an old Halloween mask," he said.

"No, I mean, how'd you get it in and out of your mouth?"

Stu patted one of the side pockets of his gigantic, puffy, Minnesota Vikings winter jacket. "I keep it in here. Then, when I blow on my hands, I put on or take off the tongue."

I had to admit it was pretty tricky.

"That's why I brought you here, Bird Bones," Stu said. "There's no such thing as a magician without a trusty assistant."

"What do you need me for? It looks like you have pretty much everything figured out."

"Drama, dude."

I agreed to do it, but only under one condition:
"Can we please go inside the school and warm up?"

That's where I was when Stu began his magic trick.
Inside. In the coatroom, to be exact.

At Babbling Brook, every grade had its own coatroom. Luckily, the windows of the eighth grade coatroom faced the flag pole. That meant I was able to
watch Stu and stay warm at the same time. Honestly,
I didn't know how Stu had convinced so many kids to
stay outside for his magic trick. Maybe it was the fact
the he wasn't wearing a jacket that caught their attention. He'd left it in the coatroom with me. At the exact
right moment, when Stu looked my way, it was going to
be my job to bring the coat out to him.

"Seriously, dude," Stu had said to me. "Take your
time when you do it. The more I shiver, the more sus-
pense there will be."

Of course, I had no intention of taking my time.
Stu would risk just about anything, I knew, if it meant
more drama—even frostbite. Or hypothermia. In any
case, whatever Stu was doing or saying, it was working.

It seemed like every kid in the school had gathered
by that flagpole. Every kid except for me, of course. And,
as it turned out, except for Justin "Just Rich" Richards.
Which wasn't surprising. Justin was a great guy, but he
was one of those kids who lived almost entirely in his
own world. I'm not trying to be mean, but kids who live
in their own worlds often have trouble functioning in

our world. Do you know the kinds of kids I'm talking about? They're the ones who routinely forget to pack shoes in their backpacks and have to walk around all day in their winter boots. They're the kids who have their names written on everything, even their socks and underwear, because their parents know they'll lose those things if they don't. Honestly, how does someone lose underwear? Or just one sock? If it sounds like I'm making fun of this kind of kid, I assure you I'm not. These kids are often totally content living in their worlds; they aren't embarrassed at all when a teacher holds up their underwear and reads their name to the rest of the class. And, really, what's so bad about that? I wish I felt good enough about myself to not get embarrassed. Anyway, Justin was that kind of kid.

On that particular morning, he must have been doing some serious daydreaming, because I watched him walk past the huge crowd of kids without even noticing they were there. A few seconds later he joined me in the coat room and hung up his coat.

"Hey, Justin," I said. My words must have startled him out of his daydream. He looked around with a confused smile on his face.

"Where is everybody?" he asked.

"You just passed them," I said. "They're all out there." I pointed out the window.

"How come?" he asked.

"Stu is performing a magic trick."

"Really? I love magic!" Justin quickly put his coat back on and headed back outside. Or at least I thought he had put his coat on. I was busy watching for Stu's signal so I didn't actually see Justin until he was outside again. When I spotted him wandering into the crowd, I saw I had been mistaken. Justin wasn't wearing his coat. The coat he was wearing was huge, and puffy, and Minnesota Vikings themed. That's right. He was wearing Stu's coat. How this could have happened, I still can't fully explain. Besides not looking anything alike, the coats were completely different sizes. Stu was practically a giant, after all. Justin? He was barely taller than I was. Did Justin not realize the jacket he was currently wearing went down past his knees? It was at that moment that Stu looked straight at me and nodded.

What was I supposed to do? Chase after Justin, maybe? No, he'd already disappeared into the crowd. I tried shaking my head at Stu, and mouthing through the glass that I didn't have his coat. But he must not have understood, because he nodded his head more emphatically and kept talking to the crowd. I knew Stu well enough to know he would keep talking, keep stalling, until I brought out the jacket. And honestly, the kid looked really cold. His arms had gone from red to ghost white. He needed a jacket. Any jacket. I grabbed Justin's small, only-sorta-puffy, green and yellow coat and raced out of the building.

As I worked my way through the crowd, I heard Stu making up stuff about his magic jacket.

"The jacket I'm about to wear has been covered in Himalayan lizard spit," he explained through chattering teeth.

"Ew," someone said. But Stu kept going. "Scientists recently discovered this saliva has amazing physical properties. For instance, it doesn't freeze even when subjected to extreme cold. Its airborne scent—"

"Here you go, Stu," I said when I arrived.

I held it out for him to see, but he didn't look. For the sake of drama, I guess, he kept his eyes locked on the crowd as he held out his arms. He wanted me to put the jacket on for him.

"Through the miracle of magic," Stu said, "the wearer of this coat is endowed with all the mystical powers of that sacred mountain range. Gaze in wonder, dudes and dudettes, as I defy natural science by placing my tongue upon this pole . . . and taking it off again!" Stu waved his hands dramatically as the crowd gasped.

It was only then, I think, that he realized he was wearing the wrong jacket. The sleeves barely made it past his elbows.

I spotted Justin Richards in the crowd. He was staring up at Stu, totally captivated—but I'm pretty sure he still hadn't noticed his mistake.

For some reason, Stu patted the jacket's pockets. I'm not certain if he did this because he actually thought I'd managed to put the fake tongue in there, or because he didn't know what else to do.

I felt bad.

I wasn't sure how I could have possibly predicted Justin's mistake, but still: I'd let Stu down. Without that rubber tongue, he obviously wasn't going to be able to perform his magic trick. The other kids would walk away, cold and angry and disappointed.

Or that's what I thought—until Stu turned and licked the pole anyway.

Of course, that was only the first part of the "trick." The second part, the real part, was taking the tongue back off the pole.

Stu leaned back, his tongue stretching out of his mouth.

He leaned back more.

The tongue stayed stuck on the pole.

He straightened up again. Then, just like when he was rehearsing earlier in the morning, he put his booted foot on the pole to get some more leverage.

Only this time he wasn't pretending.

He was trying to pull his actual tongue off the pole.

He pushed off with his boot. He leaned back with his upper body. He jerked back his head.

His tongue stretched and then . . . finally . . . came off the pole.

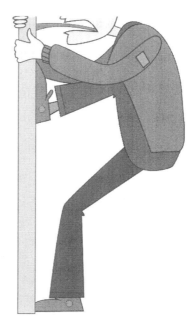

Or most of it did, anyway.

Stu turned to the crowd and said, "Abracadabra."

At least he tried to. He couldn't pronounce the word very well—not with all the blood gushing out.

(Luckily, with time, the tongue healed. I wish I could say this was the worst injury he sustained while trying to become legendary, but it wasn't. Soon he would sustain much, much worse.)

Stu Becomes a Jedi Knight

That winter was the first time I went to Stu's house. Honestly, I didn't know what to expect. I mean, Stu's HOUSE? The possibilities were endless. A house of mirrors, perhaps? A castle with a moat? As it turned out, Stu's house looked totally normal. The house was located about four normal blocks from school, in a normal neighborhood, surrounded by other normal houses. Like all the normal houses in the normal neighborhood, you had to walk up some fairly-steep-but-nothing-too-out-of-the-ordinary stairs to get to the front door.

I was in front of Stu as we climbed the stairs.

By the way, I've always thought it was weird how we describe walking up stairs as *climbing* them. It makes me think of scaling a mountain. I mean, climbing should involve the use of all four limbs, shouldn't it?

I stepped under the awning and stepped aside for Stu to open the door. Except, when I turned around, Stu wasn't there.

Well, Stu's upper body wasn't there.

His feet and legs dangled from the awning.

"Stu?" I said. "What are you doing?"

"Going into the house, Bird Bones." He said this as though what he was doing was as normal as his house.

His legs disappeared as he pulled himself all the way on top of the awning. Now this was what climbing was supposed to look like.

I took a few steps back so I could see him. There was a partly open window above the awning and Stu pried it open with his fingers.

"Wouldn't it be easier to go through the front door?" I hollered up to him.

But by now he was already crawling headfirst through the window. I only had a few seconds to wonder what I was supposed to do—I was way too short to reach the awning—when the front door opened.

"Sorry for the wait, dude," Stu said. "The front door was locked."

"Ever heard of a key?" I asked.

"Why would I need a key, Bird Bones, when I can climb up the awning?"

Once again, he said this as though he was being completely logical.

And actually, it sort of was logical, from a kid's point of view. What self-respecting kid chooses to walk into a house if he or she can climb into it?

But what about from an adult's point of view?

Did his parents realize he didn't have a key? Did they realize he left a window partly open during the day? My parents would have killed me if I did that. I could almost hear them telling me I might as well invite robbers into our home.

That's what I was thinking about as I stepped inside and realized that, sure enough, Stu's place had been robbed.

The living room was to my right, and it was almost completely empty. Still, it was clear that stuff had been in there before. The carpet had indentations from where a couch must have been. A TV stand had a few cords resting on it but no TV.

To my left was a staircase. On the wall next to it were squares of lighter paint.

Picture frames, I thought. There used to be picture frames there.

"Dude, you coming to my room or what?" Stu was at the top of the staircase. As always, his voice was casual.

"Stu," I said, "I think your house has been robbed!"

"Obviously it's been robbed, Bird Bones," he said, his voice still casual. "Didn't you see the TV stand without a TV on it?"

"Why aren't you freaking out about this?" I asked. "I mean, how do you know the robbers aren't still in the house?"

Stu waved the idea off. "After all these years? I think I would have noticed."

"All these years? What are you talking about?"

And that's when Stu explained how he had literally invited a robber into his home.

The first thing Stu told me was that both his parents were in the military. This meant they were gone a lot. It also meant he was on his own a lot.

It had been that way since he was a little kid.

Supposedly his aunt was in charge of him while his parents were gone, but she didn't really see the point. Like his parents, she thought he was more than capable of taking care of himself.

"But you were only a little kid," I reminded him.

Stu just shrugged. "I was already really tall, dude," he said. "I guess they figured if I looked kind of like an adult, I might as well be an adult."

Anyway, he didn't mind. Having a house to himself when he was only seven or eight years old was kind of cool.

Besides, he didn't actually spend much time in the house. During the day he'd usually be outside playing with his *Star Wars* action figures.

"That's probably how he knew I liked *Star Wars*, Bird Bones," Stu told me. "He probably saw me out there, day after day, on my own."

"Who's *he*?" I asked him.

"The dude who showed up at my house one night."

On the night in question, Stu opened his front door and found some guy in a cloak standing in front of him. Half his face was covered by a giant hood. When Stu asked him why he was wearing this cloak, the guy said, "Because I'm a Jedi Knight."

Then he asked Stu if he wanted to become a Jedi Knight too.

"Talk about a no-brainer, dude," Stu told me.

"So you let him in your house?"

"I was eight, dude. A guy was standing at my door offering to train me to be a Jedi Knight. *Of course* I let him in my house."

They spent the night "training," which meant they spent the night fighting with broomsticks. When Stu asked the Jedi Knight why he didn't have a lightsaber, he said it had shorted out recently and was in the shop.

"Which seemed to make sense at the time," Stu said.

Especially when the guy asked him if he wanted a lightsaber of his own.

"Another no-brainer," Stu told me.

The guy told him he could get the lightsaber for him, no problem. But it was going to cost a lot of money. It was a lightsaber, after all.

"Which also made sense," Stu said.

Stu explained to his Jedi Master that he didn't have much money because he was just a kid. The Jedi thought about this for a while. Or pretended to think about it, anyway. This moment was actually the whole reason he'd put on the cloak. "What about all this stuff?" he said to Stu. "Maybe I could trade it in for a lightsaber."

When he said "all this stuff," he really meant *all* of it.

Not just the TV, the couch, and some picture frames, but also a radio, the DVD player—everything.

Together, the Jedi and Stu carried these items out of the house, down the stairs, and onto the bed of a truck parked next to the curb. When they were finished, the Jedi got in the truck and said he'd order the lightsaber as soon as he could. He said it would arrive by mail, probably within four to five business days, but it was hard to know for sure. After all, it was a *lightsaber*. It had to be specially made by a master craftsman.

Then the Jedi left.

"Well," Stu told me, "he didn't leave quite that easily. He stalled the truck a few times first. Looking back, I'm pretty sure he was an older neighbor kid down the street. I doubt he was even old enough to have his license."

"What do you mean, you *think* it was the kid down the street. Why don't you know?"

"He had the hood on, dude. Besides, I didn't want him to be just some normal kid. I made myself believe he was an actual Jedi Knight."

"So then what happened?" I asked.

"I didn't get the lightsaber, dude, if that's what you mean."

It wasn't. "No, I mean, did you tell your parents? Did the kid get caught?"

Stu shook his head. It was months until his parents returned home and saw everything was missing. By then, the Jedi's family had moved. They could have tried to track the guy down, but the truth was that they were angrier with Stu than with some teenager they'd never met. After all, he'd been duped as though he was some stupid little kid.

"You *were* some stupid little kid," I pointed out.

"I wasn't little," Stu reminded me, as if that mattered.

As punishment, his parents refused to replace any of the stuff that had been stolen. That way, the emptiness would remind him every day what he had done.

I told Stu that seemed pretty harsh. Did the punishment really teach him a lesson?

Stu shrugged. "Not really, dude," he admitted. "I mean, obviously it was stupid of me to let that guy into the house. But for a while I really believed that I was going to get that lightsaber. Which was pretty great, you know? Every day I'd walk to the mailbox and think a lightsaber was gonna be in there. A *lightsaber*, Bird Bones. How cool is that?"

Stu looked around his empty house and shrugged again.

"Even though I never got the lightsaber, dude, just getting to believe I was going to get one was worth way more than any of this stuff."

How I Became a Football Star (Briefly, But Still)

As always during recess, I was sitting at the edge of the playground. As always, Stu was nowhere to be found. As always, Clara was on the tire swing, her feet planted firmly on the ground.

Once again, a football fell out of the sky. This time it landed to my left and bounced toward the giant yellow slide.

It never got there, though, because a foot stopped it.

A giant foot.

Stu's foot.

I'd been looking for him for at least ten minutes, and hadn't seen him. How did he just appear like that? Where had he come from? To this day I can't explain it.

"A little help?" It was Chad Logan's voice. He had apparently decided not to come all the way to the playground this time, and I didn't blame him. Last time he made the trip, his return was painful, slippery, and embarrassing.

Stu bent his long body and picked up the ball. "Play you for it, dude," he said.

"What?"

Yeah—what?

"If you win, you can have your football. If we win, we get to keep the football."

"Who's we?" Chad Logan asked.

Yeah—who was we?

"Me and Bird Bones," Stu said.

"That's it?" Chad said. "Just you and Bird Bones?"

It sounded like that's exactly what he meant. "Wait," I said. "Stu. I don't—"

"I'm in."

I turned. It was Clara. She stood up and set her book on the now-wobbling tire. I think this was her way of marking her territory. *Just because I'm not here*, she seemed to be saying, *doesn't mean anyone's allowed to take my spot.*

"You, Bird Bones, and Clarasil," Chad said. "That makes three."

"I want to play too!"

I turned some more. It was Justin Richards. Stumpy, mind-wandering, almost-as-short-as-I-was Justin Richards.

"You, Bird Bones, Clarasil, and Just Rich." Chad smirked. "Anyone else?"

"Me."

We all turned and found some little kid stepping away from a slide and heading in our direction. He couldn't have been more than a fourth grader.

"Me too!"

"Me too!"

"Can I play?"

"How about me? Can I play too?"

Shouts came from all over the playground. Within a few seconds, a whole line of elementary school kids stood next to me.

I looked at Stu. He still held the football in one hand. The other hand rubbed his chin.

"All of us," he said, "versus all of you."

The whole thing was pretty inspirational. I'd been hoping to play football at recess for years, and now I was going to get my chance.

I should have been excited, but when I looked at our competition I realized I'd never really thought the situation through. Our opponents seemed suddenly huge.

They were just guys from my class—I knew that. But, compared to most of us, they might as well have been NFL linemen.

"Let's get this over with, Chad," one of them hollered.

"We'll pummel them and then we'll take our ball back," said another.

Chad considered it. Then he smiled. "We'll do it if you promise not to cry to a teacher when we're done."

I, for one, couldn't promise anything of the sort. What did they mean by *pummel* us? That didn't sound like touch football. And we weren't playing on snow here. We weren't even playing on grass. This was ice. Slick, thick ice. Getting pummeled would hurt badly enough on a regular surface. But on this stuff? *No way,*

I thought. *The only reason I'm not going to cry is because I'm not going to play.*

"You're on," Stu said.

That's when all the other puny elementary kids let out a battle bellow. Well, it was more like a battle squeal. But still, their courage was impressive. I've never been one to be ashamed of cowardice—not if it's justified. Stupid courage is just that—stupid. But then again, even I had standards. I didn't need to be as brave as your average middle schooler, but I did need to be as brave as your average fourth grader. Besides, how dangerous could this really be? Stu was the one who came up with the challenge, so it was fair to assume he'd be the one with the ball most of the time. He was plenty skinny, so there was a chance he'd be snapped in two. But he was also almost seven feet tall, so you couldn't really say he was at a size disadvantage.

Maybe the eighth graders wouldn't be able to catch up to Stu's long-legged strides, I thought.

Even if they did catch up to him, well, he brought this on himself. If he wanted the football so badly, he could have it.

"Okay, team," Stu said after our team huddled up. "When in doubt, get the ball to Bird Bones."

"What are you talking about?" I said.

"Relax, dude—you'll do great."

"Why don't you take the ball?"

"On this ice? No way, dude."

"You're the one who got us all into this!" I protested.

"My legs are too long, Bird Bones. I won't be able to stop or change directions without falling. But your

74

puny legs are perfect for this terrain. Your steps are so itty bitty you probably won't even notice you're on ice."

I think he meant that as a compliment.

In any case, he wasn't kidding. Stu tossed me the ball on the first play and, well, to this day I can't explain it.

Except to say Stu was right.

I ran around five or six guys before anyone touched me. The same thing happened on the next play. You know that scene in one of the *Star Wars* movies when the Empire's big, hulking four-legged metal contraptions are tripped up by the Alliance's little fighter jets? That's exactly what this felt like. I was a fighter jet as the other team stumbled and fell like they were made of rusted metal. I'd been so worried I'd get splatted on the ice, but they were the ones going *SPLAT*!

"Everyone," Chad finally ordered, "get Bird Bones! He's their only player!"

That's when Stu faked the handoff to me and threw the ball instead. Clara Berns was wide open. After she caught the ball, she could have walked the rest of the way past the cone that marked the end zone. But she didn't. Clara kept running until she crossed the goal line. Just as I'd suspected, she was really, really fast.

I'd like to tell you this was a true Cinderella story. But that would be dishonest. There was no great upset. David didn't beat Goliath.

We lost. By more than one touchdown.

The eighth grade guys got to keep their ball and their field.

But we didn't get pummeled. At least not literally.

All of us walked away relatively unharmed. We even scored a few more touchdowns. When one of the little kids scored, he spiked the ball and did an end-zone dance that lasted several minutes. When Just Rich wandered with the ball into the end zone, he just kept on wandering twenty, thirty, forty more yards. I don't think he would have stopped wandering if we hadn't chased him down and brought him back to the field.

No, we didn't win, but it felt almost like we did.

Clara even high-fived me.

"I didn't know anyone could run on ice like that, Patrick," she said.

Then she walked back to the playground to get her book.

I didn't know you knew my name, I thought.

Stu Enters People's Thoughts

It was a few weeks before Valentine's Day, and love must've already been in the air. Anyway, *something* must have been in the air. Whatever it was, Melissa Crabtree breathed it in. And then she sneezed it out.

This wasn't just any sneeze, either; it was a seismic eruption of phlegm and spit. And it hit Matt McCoy full on the side of the face.

I don't know why she sneezed right on him, but my guess is that it was habit. When you're sitting in rows, the person in the most danger of getting sneezed on is in front of you. The polite thing to do is to turn your head to the side and into the crook of your arm. Melissa turned her head to her side, but didn't have time to bring her arm to her face. Honestly, it was probably a good thing she didn't raise her arm. The sneeze might have blown the arm right off. Unfortunately, in Ms. Gribbs's class we didn't sit in rows. We sat in a circle. That meant

Matt McCoy's face was in the wrong place at the wrong time.

I don't think anyone blamed him when Matt had one of his meltdowns—not even Melissa, who now had both her arms covering her face as she apologized over and over. I'd write down what Matt was yelling if I could. But most of the words he used weren't suitable to print.

When Matt had cooled down a little, Ms. Gribbs ordered him to go see Mr. Rodine, and as usual, he didn't object. It was the weirdest thing. Matt was always having conniptions in class, but the second Ms. Gribbs mentioned Mr. Rodine's office, he'd obediently stand up and quietly leave the room.

Twenty minutes later, he returned to class calm and collected. He patted Melissa on the back and said he was sorry.

I felt a slap at my desk. When I looked down, I saw Stu had passed me a note: Who's mr· Rodine?

The counselor, I wrote back.

where is his office?

I didn't know why he was so interested, but I answered him anyway. Just down the hall.

Stu didn't ask me any more questions—but a few minutes later, when Ms. Gribbs went into her office to get something, Stu got out of his own desk and strode right out of the classroom.

A few more minutes later, Ms. Gribbs emerged from her office and noticed Stu's empty desk.

I don't know if Melissa took pity on Ms. Gribbs or if she simply couldn't handle another freak-out today, but before Ms. Gribbs could start shrieking about a missing student, Melissa said, "Stu just left and he didn't say where he was going."

This news was apparently a little bit better than Ms. Gribbs's initial assumption—that he had vanished again into thin air—because instead of shrieking she just stood there and stared at the door. I kept waiting for her to sit down, but she didn't.

After what felt like ten minutes she said, "Why would he be gone this long?"

After what felt like twenty minutes she said, "Are you sure he walked out that door?"

I guess she was still hanging on to her suspicion that he'd suddenly vanished.

After what felt like thirty minutes, she went back to her office and—for the second time that school year—reported Stuart Sanderson had gone missing.

"No," she yelled into the phone, "I'm sorry, Principal Davis, but that's simply not good enough. There must be something we can do—some way to ensure this boy's safety."

She hung up.

Then she re-emerged and said, "Attention, students. I have an announcement. The powers that be are unwilling to confront the situation we now face. Consequently, we must take matters into our own hands."

She told all of us to stand up and calmly but quickly vacate the premises. When Justin Richards asked what she meant, Ms. Gribbs said, "Go into the hallway and wait for me."

Once we were all outside she encouraged us to link arms with at least one other person—that way there was a smaller risk of us getting lost. Why she thought we were going to get lost in a school we went to every day, I don't know. Maybe a favorite student of hers really did go missing and never came back. Maybe she really did name her marker box "Janice" as a tribute to this missing girl. Or maybe Ms. Gribbs really was—to use the technical medical term—completely whacked out. Whatever the reason, she assigned us to various halls and locations in the school, wished us good luck, and released her search posse.

About half the class went one way down the hallway, and the other half went the other way. The group I was in was quiet and serious until it took a right at the next hallway. Then everyone started talking and laughing. A few guys high-fived and said, "Can you believe this? This is awesome."

I didn't blame them. There was something liberating about roaming the halls when they were completely empty. Especially since we couldn't get in trouble for doing it. If another teacher spotted us and asked where we were supposed to be, we could honestly tell him or her, "Wandering the halls."

While I didn't blame them, I didn't go with them. I watched the posse move farther and farther down the hall, and then I doubled back the way we had come. I passed our English classroom and kept moving. The other posse had done the same thing as the one I was in—when I reached another hallway, I saw them grouped together at the other end of it, deciding which way to go next.

The only one who hadn't gone with them was Clara Berns. She sat on the floor with her back against a locker, her head buried in a book.

I almost said, "Hey, Clara," but didn't, because I was afraid she'd say something like, "This spot on the floor is occupied for the remainder of English class."

Instead, I proceeded down the hallway.

When I got to Mr. Rodine's office, I wasn't surprised that the door was slightly ajar.

I nudged it open, fully expecting to see either Mr. Rodine or Stu or both.

But the room was empty.

This was the first time I'd seen the room, and I couldn't believe how comfy it looked. Unlike every other classroom at Babbling Brook, the floor in this room was covered by a soft, squishy carpet. There were two leather chairs with lots of padding, plus one of those giant rubber balls that are supposed to be good for your back or something. A small round wooden table had a laptop on it that was playing background music— it sounded like it was raining in here—and a jar with some stress balls in it.

No wonder Matt McCoy never objected to coming here. This place was great.

I'd only been here for a few minutes and I already felt soothed.

CLANG!

I looked around, startled, but didn't know what I'd just heard.

CLANG!

This time I was pretty sure the sound was coming from the far wall. As I studied this wall, I noticed the air-vent cover was hanging crookedly a few feet from the ground. The screws were missing from three of its corners, but after a second I spotted them.

They were below the vent cover, resting in some sort of indentation in the squishy carpet.

A shoeprint.

A GIANT shoeprint.

As I scanned the whole carpet I saw some more giant shoeprints. They all pointed toward the vent.

I made some indentations of my own as I walked across the room and knelt by the wall.

I thought of Stu folding himself up like origami and fitting into the podium.

Could he have...?

No—it was impossible. This was a bigger vent cover than most, but it wasn't THAT big.

CLANG!

"Stu? Are you in there?"

"No, dude."

"Oh my gosh."

"This isn't Stu, Bird Bones. It's Clara Berns's conscience."

"What?"

"I want to go to the dance with her," Stu said.

"What are you talking about?"

"The Valentine's Day dance."

I still didn't get it.

"Dude, just go get Clara and have her stand by the wall outside the office, okay?"

I *still* didn't get it.

"So she can listen to her conscience tell her to go to the dance with me," Stu said.

Later on I realized the full extent of his plan. Ms. Gribbs had sent us to look for Stu—but he had no way of knowing she'd do that. His original plan was to lay wedged in that vent until the bell rang, then wait for Clara to randomly walk by the vent. He'd decided to wait there as long as necessary.

In that moment, as far as I was concerned, he could wait forever. I hadn't told him about my love for Clara, but that didn't change the fact he was asking me to help him go to a dance with the love of my life.

"Sorry—" I started to tell Stu.

But he interrupted me. "Please, dude. Just do it. Love is at stake."

Exactly, I thought.

But then again, I had to give it to him—the guy was willing to do anything to get Clara's attention, even squeeze himself into the school's ventilation system. Whereas I wasn't even willing to say, "Hi."

Still, I wasn't about to ask her to go to a dance with him—I didn't know much about romance, but that definitely seemed counterproductive.

Talking with Clara sounded like a good idea, though. Maybe I'd even ask her to the dance myself. What was he going to do about it? He was stuck in a vent.

"Dude—"

"I'm going," I told him.

And I did. I left the soft floors of the office for the hard floors of the rest of the school. I walked down one hallway until I got to another one. The same one Clara Berns was sitting in the last time I saw her. The same one she was still sitting in now.

"Hey, Clara," I said.

She looked annoyed, as though I'd jolted her out of whatever world the book had put her in. "What now?"

I couldn't think of what to say. I couldn't possibly ask her to a dance when she was in such a crabby mood. But what else did we have to talk about? My mind was racing, spinning its wheels.

The only other thing I could think to talk about was . . . Stu.

"I'm supposed to take you somewhere."

"Huh?" She tilted her head. "Where?"

I couldn't tell if she was still annoyed but I didn't think so. She actually sounded curious.

"I can't tell you," I said.

"Are you and Stu up to something again?" she said.

"Something like that," I said.

I liked the way she implied that I—not just Stu—was always up to something. I also liked the way she reached out her hand and let me help her to her feet.

As soon as she was standing she let go of me, but as we walked I could still remember the pressure of her hand in mine.

The vent was in the next hallway, on the other side of the office, and just as we were about to turn down it, we saw Principal Davis heading in our direction.

He was looking down at his feet, which were moving briskly. By now he probably had received reports that Ms. Gribbs's students had been seen wandering the halls. He might have also needed to check on the ventilation system. Can a full-size human lodge himself into a vent without causing problems? How about a mega-size human? My guess is no.

Mr. Davis was so interested in his feet, I'm not sure he could see anything else—not even two students, Clara and me, who were standing right in front of him.

As for Stu, I'm not sure he could see anything at all.

He had been lying in that vent a long time now, his face next to the vent cover that was above us on the ceiling, the metal slats preventing him from doing much but listen. Finally, he heard the footsteps he'd been waiting for, and said, "Dude, Clara, I am your conscience. You should totally go to the Valentine's Dance with me—I mean, Stu. You should go to the dance with Stu."

Unfortunately, the footsteps didn't belong to Clara—they belonged to Principal Davis, who stopped right where he was and spun in a complete circle.

"Who said that?" he asked.

Looking back, I wish I had tried to take the blame. I wish I had said it was me—that would have been the honorable thing to do. But I didn't think about it at the time, and anyway, I don't think it would have mattered.

Principal Davis had already spotted the vent and was trying to look through one of the slats. I'm not sure what he saw, but it was enough for him to step away, march around the side of the Mr. Rodine's office to the front of it, and go inside.

After a while he and Stu emerged from the office and walked back in the direction Principal Davis had originally come.

At first I didn't think they saw Clara or me standing there, but then Principal Davis said, "Get back to class, students."

We didn't have anything else to do, so we followed Principal Davis's orders.

Several minutes later, as Clara and I sat in Ms. Gribbs's class and waited for the bell to ring, a voice came on over the intercom:

"Dude, Clara," the voice boomed, "this is your conscience. Again. And I still think you should go to the dance with Stu."

I was never entirely sure how Stu got ahold of the principal's intercom system—it must have been located in Principal Davis's office—but I also wasn't entirely surprised.

After all, the desire to become legendary has driven many mere mortals to epic feats of ambition and daring. Couple that desire with the other great ambition—*love*—and there's no telling what someone will accomplish.

Of course, someone who attempts the impossible takes risks—huge risks—and not all of them pay off. Stu was about to take a risk that would backfire big time. A risk that would make me ask the question, "Is he a hero or is his life a tragedy?"

Stu Fights
with Swords

Looking back, I honestly don't know why I wasn't more upset that Stu was in love with the love of my life.

Then again, I was almost never upset with Stu about anything.

The kid was just too likable.

He pulled a lot of pranks on a lot of people—but somehow everyone always knew he didn't mean anything by them. He wasn't trying to embarrass or humiliate or harass. He was nothing like a bully. In fact, it always felt like Stu's antics were especially designed to foil bullies at every turn.

Even when those bullies were teachers.

Which is probably why Mr. Fishly, our gym teacher, seemed so intent on killing Stu.

Don't get me wrong—Stu wasn't the only kid Mr. Fishly tried to kill. As the year went on, it became increasingly clear that he wanted all of us to die.

During gym class, if possible.

Our dodge ball games would get pretty brutal, but they were nothing compared to Monarch of the Mat. That's where Mr. Fishly had us stand on a huge, thick, cushy gymnastics mat . . . until he blew the whistle. Then it was a free-for-all. The goal was to be the last one standing on the mat, and I can still see Chad Logan flexing his beefy biceps as he chucked kids onto the not-at-all-cushy gym floor. Mr. Fishly never smiled—or showed any emotion, for that matter—but I swear you could see a gleeful glint in his eyes as he watched Chad turn human bodies into carnage. Once, a few kids tried hopping off the mat before Chad could get to them, but Mr. Fishly said they were being poor sports and ordered them to climb back up and take their punishment like men. When Lisa Miller protested she wasn't a man, Mr. Fishly responded enigmatically: "Not with that attitude you're not."

Monarch of the Mat was child's play compared to Slaughter Ball, a game that was actually just tackle football, only without the equipment . . . or the grass. Mr. Fishly would lead us across the football field to the Slaughter Ball field, which most people simply called the Babbling Brook Middle School parking lot. I'm not sure what gave Chad and Mr. Fishly more pleasure: smearing a kid across the asphalt, or setting off a car alarm by splatting someone against a side door.

I'm also not sure how he got away with playing these games. Maybe no one believed students who complained. Maybe the games were so absurdly brutal that that's exactly how parents and adults thought of them—as absurd. How could anyone take a kid seriously who claimed they were forced to play tackle football in a parking lot?

Besides, maimed wasn't the same thing as murdered. As far as I know, no kid had ever walked away from one of Mr. Fishly's gym classes with anything worse than an abrasion. For his part, Mr. Fishly didn't make his desire to truly kill us official until he brought swords to class.

"Bird Bones," Stu said to me, "we get to sword fight!"

Though he was technically only talking to me, his voice boomed as usual.

"No, Mr. Sanderson," Mr. Fishly corrected. "We're not *sword fighting*. We're *fencing*."

"Sorry, Mr. F," Stu said. Then he said, "Can I have the big sword over there?"

There were a total of three swords lying on the gym floor, and they were lined up from smallest to largest.

"It's not a *sword*," Mr. Fishly corrected. "It's a saber." His voice was stern. Evidently, he really wanted us to learn the proper terminology. One at a time, he held up the swords and made us repeat their names: the foil, the épée, the saber. Then he told us we could pick any of the three weapons.

"If you would like a chance to use the foil," he said, holding up the smallest blade, "line up over there."

No one went to where he was pointing.

"If you would like to wield the épée, stand over there."

Still no one got in line.

"If you'd like to use the saber—"

Everyone rushed into line before Mr. Fishly had a chance to finish his sentence.

"Suit yourself," he said. "I, for one, would rather brandish a more precise blade." He picked up the foil and began talking about its many virtues. It was pretty boring, to tell you the truth, and I don't think anybody was really listening.

Nobody, anyway, except Justin Richards, who typically lived in a fantasy world of his own that likely included not only swords but dragons too. "Where'd you learn all that stuff?" he asked Mr. Fishly.

"Night school," Mr. Fishly said.

Or that's what I thought he said.

"You can take night classes on fencing?" Justin asked.

Or that's what I thought he asked.

"It's a fair point, Mr. Richards," Mr. Fishly said. "Technically, a knight didn't fence. This form of dueling appeared much later on. But my training included a wide variety of fighting skills besides Dark Age combat."

That's when I understood what they were talking about: Mr. Fishly didn't go to night school; he went to *knight* school.

"So . . ." Justin said, "you're a real knight?"

Mr. Fishly nodded. I imagined him on his knee while wearing chainmail. His perfectly-round bald spot gleamed as a sword tapped him on each shoulder. "I was knighted by Larry, Lord of Rapid River," he said, "not a fortnight ago."

There was something weird about the comment, and it wasn't just the fake accent he used or the odd phrasing. That name, *Larry, Lord of Rapid River* . . .

"Dude," Stu boomed to me and everyone else, "Mr. F works at Darke Ages!"

Of course! A few months ago, Larry Bierman opened Darke Ages, a medieval-themed restaurant on the other side of town. Before that, he'd been the owner of a car dealership located in the exact place the restaurant now stood. Unfortunately, his change in business hadn't improved his TV ads. Darke Ages, Lord Larry exclaimed during commercial breaks, provided "non-stop festival fun!" and offered "authentic medieval grubbe!" These phrases popped up on the screen as he shouted them, and a bunch of the words had extra letters at the end, an attempt to look like Old English, I guess.

The rest of the class must have been thinking of those commercials too, because some of them chuckled.

Mr. Fishly didn't see what was so funny. "That is correct, Mr. Sanderson. I earn my grubbe by wielding weaponry from six to eight Thursday through Sunday." You could almost hear the extra letters in *grubbe*.

He made a few slashes through the air with the foil.

"Is that how you got those swords?" Justin asked.

Mr. Fishly nodded his head. "Lord Larry bestowed them upon me when I vanquished my foes."

I was pretty sure that was a yes, but Justin wasn't as convinced. "What does that mean?" he asked.

"It means, Mr. Richards, I acquire these swords when I best my adversaries."

Justin still must have been confused, because he started to ask, "What does that mean?" again.

Mr. Fishly cut him off. "Let me show you," he said.

In one quick move he put the blade of the foil he was holding under the blade of the saber and flipped the saber off the floor and into the air. The saber's handle landed perfectly in Justin's outstretched right hand.

Even Justin knew what to do next. He brought the sword down to his waist and pointed it at Mr. Fishly.

"En garde," Mr. Fishly said.

I had to admit, the whole flipping-the-sword thing had been pretty impressive. And maybe I should have been impressed with what happened next, too, but I wasn't.

I was too scared.

Mr. Fishly made several slashes with his sword, and just like that, Justin was on the ground, writhing in pain.

The saber was once again on the floor, where Justin had dropped it, but not for long: Mr. Fishly flipped it to the next person in line. "En garde!"

Before Mark Bennett knew what was happening, the sword was out of his hand and he had joined Justin on the floor. It was only at this point—with Mark groaning in pain and Mr. Fishly flipping the sword to the next person in line—that I realized the blades, thank goodness, weren't sharp. Maybe it was the fact that neither Mark nor Justin appeared to be bleeding that tipped me off; or maybe it was my common sense kicking in. Mr. Fishly couldn't actually be *stabbing* students—could he?

Fortunately not. As I looked closer at the blade I saw that, sure enough, it was rounded off at the end.

I breathed a sigh of relief, but only a slight one. A lack of blood didn't mean a lack of pain.

Mr. Fishly slashed his sword and Nissa Andrews shrieked in agony. The next one up was Lindsay Erdle, then Josh Lammers, then Kelsey Bray. Mr. Fishly lunged and lashed; he juked and jabbed. One by one the members of my gym class were left yelping as the saber went skittering across the floor.

I shouldn't have minded when Chad Logan got the same treatment from Mr. Fishly. After the delight he'd taken in hurling me off mats and into cars, I should have been happy to watch Mr. Fishly hack away at his limbs. But as Chad cussed and even cried a little, I couldn't bring myself to smile at his suffering. After all, I was still in line; soon I'd be the one trying to hold back the tears.

If anything, I was in greater danger than Chad or anyone else: As the shortest kid in the class, I presented a lower target than the others. Mr. Fishly might swipe at my wrist but slash my throat instead.

I was imagining myself sobbing on the floor when I heard Mr. Fishly raise his voice. "I said 'En garde,' Mr. Sanderson."

Bringing my attention back to the gym, I saw it was Stu's turn to hold the saber, and he was doing just that, but weirdly so: his arm stretched straight in front of him, the sword held parallel to the ground. "I heard you, Mr. F," Stu said.

"That means we both need to bend our arms so we can clink blades," Mr. Fishly said.

"You can bend your arm, Mr. F, but I think I'm going to keep mine the way it is."

"You can't!"

Mr. Fishly's voice sounded surprisingly childish. In fact, he *looked* surprisingly childish. At about 5'9", he was at least a foot taller than yours truly, and at least a couple inches taller than everyone else—except, of course, for Stu. Next to Stuart Sanderson, Mr. Fishly appeared positively shrimpy. Of course, he *wasn't* next to Stu—that was the issue. Stu's wingspan, as you can imagine, was practically endless, and by refusing to bend his arm, he was able to keep our sword-fighting gym teacher a comfortable distance away. Mr. Fishly had a beer belly, a goatee, and a balding head, but he looked at that moment like a kid who wanted cookies just out of his reach.

When he said, "This isn't how you're supposed to fight!" he sounded like he was having a tantrum.

Stu didn't say anything, but he didn't move his arm, either.

"If you insist on doing this, I'll have to fail you in the fencing unit," Mr. Fishly said.

Stu was never too worried about his grades, so I wasn't surprised when he didn't do as he was told.

"Standing like that is dangerous, Mr. Sanderson," Mr. Fishly said. "In just one or two moves I could break your arm."

Still Stu didn't flinch. The whiny tone of Mr. Fishly's voice made me suspect he was bluffing. I highly doubted he could actually break Stu's arm from where he stood— or, even if he could, that he would announce his intentions before carrying them out. How he'd kept his job this long was beyond me, but he'd *have* to get fired if he told a kid he was going to break his arm and then did exactly that. Wouldn't he? Then again, the man was having a tizzy fit right in front of us—so maybe his job security wasn't a top priority. Maybe any second now he would slash and stab and—*crack!*—Stu's arm would hang limply from his side.

Luckily, the class bell made the decision for him. It rang and Stu took a few long strides backward before dropping the sword on the ground and continuing to reverse his way out the door.

As we stood in the hallway together, I told Stu I was surprised he'd escaped with his life and limbs intact.

Stu just shrugged his shoulders and asked me what day of the week it was.

"Thursday—why?"

"No reason, Bird Bones," Stu said. "You wouldn't happen to be in the mood for some authentic medieval grubbe, would you?"

You could almost hear the extra letters in the way he said it.

"Welcome, Noble Peasants!" the parking-lot sign said. "Get a Royal Dinner for Only $6.99!"

"Looks like fun," my mother said. "Sure you don't want some parental supervision?"

"Positive." I opened my passenger-side door. "Thanks for the ride, Mom."

Not so long ago, the parking lot had been filled with cars that had price tags painted on their windshields. Now it was the asphalt that was painted. Spray-painted swords and shields pointed me toward "the castle," a building that had kept its off-white paint job but had added turrets and spires and several flags fluttering in the breeze. The cement front walkway had been replaced with a "drawbridge"—really just some chains and a few planks of wood. Wrapping around the castle was a "moat": a plaster pathway that had been painted blue and was cluttered with smiling, also-plaster monsters. It was odd to be walking across a blue moat when in reality it was still winter. Even if the monsters had been real, they would have been frozen in place.

"Hey, dude," Stu bellowed. He was striding on top of the moat's "water," his long legs stepping over the monsters as though they weren't even there.

"What are we doing here, Stu?" I asked him after he arrived at the drawbridge.

"I told you, Bird Bones, we're getting some grubbe."

"That's all?"

"What else would we do?" He looked at me as if I might actually be scheming some plan, as if he, Stuart Sanderson, seeker of legendary status, had never until that moment considered the possibility of doing anything at this restaurant castle other than ordering the Royal Special. "You coming, dude?"

It wasn't until I'd shrugged my shoulders and said, "I guess so," that I realized he'd turned the wrong way. Instead of stepping onto the drawbridge and joining me in line he'd pivoted around and continued walking on the moat.

"Where are you going?" I asked.

"Line's too long, Bird Bones. Let's use the back door."

By the back door, it turned out he was talking about the kitchen door—the one with a giant dumpster next to it; the one for employees only.

"We can't go in there," I said.

"Why not?"

Stu looked at me the same innocent way he had next to the drawbridge, as if he honestly didn't understand what I was talking about. "What do you mean 'why not'? This is the *kitchen* door. It's—"

Just then the door opened and I was tempted to dart behind the dumpster. Before I could, a man came clanging through the door.

No, not a man—a *knight*.

In full armor.

Okay, we were at Darke Ages, so maybe I should have been expecting to see this sort of thing—but I wasn't. Not outside. Not this close.

The knight lifted the front of his helmet to get a better look at us. That's when it occurred to me that the knight was no more than a pimply-faced teenager. "I don't think you're supposed to be back here," he said, his voice squeaking. I turned to leave, but Stu didn't budge. "Oh, well," the knight said. "I'm not supposed to be back here, either. No knights in the kitchen. I think they're afraid we're going to steal the food." He sat down on the top step with a series of clanks. "When I said I'd be a knight I thought it would be fun," he squeaked, apparently talking to himself. "Getting paid to wear armor and fight? Having adults call me *Sir* Tony?" He looked up at us. "Sounds pretty awesome, right?"

"Absolutely, dude," Stu said.

"Well, no one told me I'd have to fight against *him*." Sir Tony grabbed a metal-plated arm and grimaced.

"Who?" I asked.

"The Black Fish. The rest of us are just pretending, but that guy, I swear he *likes* hurting people."

The Black *Fish*? Likes hurting people? No doubt about it, this definitely rang a bell. "Do you mean Mr. Fishly?" I asked.

Sir Tony nodded his head so hard his mask fell in front of his face. He lifted it and said, "That's him: Sir Fishly of Babbling Brook. That guy's a psycho."

"He's our gym teacher," I said, grunting in agreement.

Sir Tony shook his head empathetically. "Tough break," he squeaked. "I'd get as far away from here as possible, if I were you. Why get anywhere near that nutcase when you don't have to?"

It seemed like sound advice.

"Mind if we use this door, dude?" Stu asked.

Sir Tony looked up at him, baffled. "Did you hear what I just said?" Tony croaked. "The safest course of action is to head back wherever you came from." When Stu didn't budge, Sir Tony finally shrugged his shoulders and gave us directions so we could sneak through the kitchen without being caught.

Stu didn't bother stepping around the teenage knight—he stepped over him.

"You coming, Bird Bones?" he said to me.

It turned out Stu wasn't lying about wanting to eat at Darke Ages. He ordered not one but two Royal Dinners—each for the peasant price of $6.99. The meal included mashed potatoes, corn, a soda of one's choice, and a huge turkey drumstick. I don't know if real knights actually ate any of this, but I had to admit it was good grubbe. There was something deeply satisfying about gnawing away at that turkey drumstick.

Stu had one drumstick in each hand and was alternating bites when a voice crackled through the restaurant. "Laaaaaadies and gentlemen! Welcome to the primary festivity!" There was a large speaker hanging from the wall above us and that's where I looked first. It took me a second to turn my gaze to the giant ring in the middle of the restaurant. "Some of you have already witnessed tonight the captivating brutality of hand-to-hand combat," the guy with the microphone said, a weird purple hat flopping around on his head. Maybe people in the middle ages really did don purple hats, but I seriously doubted they wore sunglasses with them. "Now you shall observe the majestic violence of jousting!"

There was some scattered applause.

"As always," the man continued, waving his arms behind him, "Lord Larry shall award the victor the loser's lance."

Lord Larry waved from a throne in what looked like a press box maybe thirty feet above the ring. He wore a huge crown and a red velvet cape, as well as a polo shirt that just barely made it over his big belly. On either side of him were beautiful women, both in crowns and halter-tops, both way younger than he was. I wasn't sure how we were supposed to view this configuration. Was one the queen and one the princess? Were they both princesses? Were they both queens?

"And now," the guy with the microphone blared, "let's meet our competitors!" The lights instantly dimmed, and the cheering got a little louder. "First, our reigning champion in every combat category, the Black Fish himself, Sir Fishly of Babbling Brook!"

A spotlight shone on one end of the ring. There "Sir" Fishly was, all in black. His horse was black, as was his armor. He took his helmet off and held it in the air triumphantly as his horse reared and people cheered and booed. Others puckered their lips together and pressed their hands to their faces, apparently making themselves look like fish. I wasn't sure whether these people were mocking Mr. Fishly or supporting him.

"Now let's hear some noise for his competitor!" the man said, his floppy hat flopping. The applause went away. Several people actually turned back to their meals. "Some of you saw him try his luck with a sword earlier tonight, only to get filleted by the Black Fish— but here he is again, ready for revenge . . . Sir Tony of Pine Valley!"

The spotlight swerved to the other end of the ring, where apparently Sir Tony was supposed to make his entrance.

No one was there.

"I said," yelled the guy with the microphone, "Sir Tony of Pine Valley!"

Still no one appeared.

That's when a different voice boomed through the restaurant—only this one wasn't aided by a microphone.

"Dude, I'll get him!" Stu dropped his drumsticks and galloped toward the kitchen.

Ten minutes later, Sir Tony still hadn't arrived. All eyes had been on Stu when he promised to retrieve the missing knight: we'd watched him blast through the kitchen door, and—for a while—we'd waited anxiously for the door to open once again. But then people laughed off the strange incident and returned to their meals.

I did the same. If Stu wanted to try to convince some poor, pimply kid to re-enter the ring and get slayed by a psychopath, that was his business. My business, as far as I was concerned, was to continue gnawing away at my drumstick.

The lights came back on, and Lord Larry pulled himself out of his throne. Using his own microphone, he apologized to everyone for the delay and asked us to be patient. "Another knight has agreed to drive here and take on the dreaded Black Fish," he assured us. "That puts the new start time for the joust at about 8:30 or—"

NNNNAAAAAYYYY!

I followed Lord Larry's eyes to the end of the ring. A white horse was kicking its front hooves in the air and making large stallion snorts. Astride the horse was a knight—only unlike "Sir" Fishly, this knight didn't remove his helmet.

"Sir Tony," Lord Larry said, "glad you finally made it." His voice sounded both irritated and relieved. "In that case, let the games begin!"

A few minutes later, the princesses/queens sauntered into the ring, each holding a lance. The one holding the black lance strolled in her skirt and heels to the end of the dusty ring where "Sir" Fishly had once again emerged. The other princess/queen went to the other end and gave the knight his white lance.

Or she tried to.

Apparently, she was too short to reach the lance up to him—even though her legs looked plenty tall, as did her heels. That's when it hit me: maybe she *wasn't* too short; perhaps the knight was too tall.

I watched the knight lean to take the lance, and I noticed the armor didn't fit right. The farther he leaned, the less cover the armor provided. As he reached for the lance, I could see his wrist. As he bent over, I could see pink fabric.

Hadn't Stu been wearing a pink shirt today? The one that said, "Thanks A Lot, Red Sock!"? The one that only Stu could possibly get away with wearing?

Maybe you're thinking you saw this coming from a mile away. Maybe you're telling yourself you knew Stu was going to end up fighting Mr. Fishly the second he said he wanted to eat at Darke Ages.

If so, good for you. But before you accuse me of being dimwitted, I'd be willing to bet *nobody* in that restaurant suspected a thing. Not the customers, who were once again clapping and cheering, not Lord Larry, who yelled, "Ready, set, go!" And not Mr. Fishly, who pressed his heels into his horse and charged across the ring.

At some point, Mr. Fishly *did* figure out what was going on—probably when he saw how the knight was holding his lance. Stu's long arm was stretched straight out in front of him. The lance must have been about fifteen feet long on its own, and Stu's arm added another four or five feet.

Mr. Fishly, whose arm and lance were tucked under his armpit, likely noticed Stu's outstretched lance and had the same flashback to gym class I was currently having. I may have been watching the horses' hooves kick up clouds of dust as they raced toward one another, but I was thinking about what had happened this morning.

You can't do that, Mr. Fishly had said. But Stu hadn't listened.

You'll get a bad grade, he'd said—and still Stu hadn't budged his arm an inch.

I could break your arm, he'd said—and it was this last threat that scared me the most.

I wasn't sure whether fencing with an outstretched arm was dangerous, but it seemed likely that jousting that way would be. The two knights were gaining speed. Forty yards separated them—then thirty-five—then twenty-five. Still Stu's arm stretched straight. There was

no question his lance was going to make contact first—
but at what cost? In gym, I'd reassured myself that
Mr. Fishly wouldn't break Stu's arm because he'd get in
huge trouble. Besides losing his job, he could probably
get sued, even imprisoned. But here? He could simply
say he was *doing* his job. He could claim he had no idea
it was Stu inside the armor.

Fifteen yards left.

Ten.

I covered my eyes with my hands, spread out my
fingers. I couldn't look—but I had to.

Would the bone actually snap? Would I hear a crack?

Five yards . . . four . . . three . . . two . . .

Right then, right before Stu's lance reached
Mr. Fishly's chest, right before Stu's arm was or was not
shattered, the fearsome Black Fish dove off his horse
and out of the way. He soared for a while and thudded
for longer, flopping around in the dust like a beached
fish.

Stu was still wearing the armor as we stood outside
Darke Ages and waited for our rides home. He was in
no hurry to take it off.

"Maybe I'll wear it tomorrow for fencing class," he
said.

"Something tells me Mr. Fishly isn't going to have
us fence tomorrow, Stu."

"I hope you're wrong, dude."

"Why?"

At this point, Stu didn't have anything else to prove,
did he? I mean, he'd already won *two* standoffs in one
day. I visualized, for about the hundredth time in the

last half hour, Mr. Fishly flopping in the sandy ring. It was an image I planned to keep with me for the rest of my life.

"Because," Stu said, "I want to try sword fighting with *this*!"

He held up the black lance—the lance that used to belong to the Black Fish; the lance that Lord Larry presented to tonight's jousting champion; the lance that was now the proud property of Sir Stu, gobbler of grubbe and fighter of physical education teachers.

How Stu Got the Name "Dirt Clod"

It was around this time that Ms. Gribbs didn't show up for class. Looking back, I bet she needed a break from Stu's antics. But if that was it, she picked a bad day to miss, because for some reason Stu was gone that day too.

Ms. Gribbs's absence meant we had a substitute teacher. Usually, having a sub was a scary proposition.

For the sub, I mean.

The combination of Stu trying to be legendary and Chad Logan trying to be a terrifying bully was bad enough. What made it even worse was that subs didn't have any lessons planned to keep the rest of us focused. It didn't take long for anarchy to reign.

But this sub was different. For one thing, he'd taken the time to reorganize the desks. Instead of the giant circle Ms. Gribbs preferred, the sub had put the desks into rows. It was a small thing, but it let us know right off the bat that he meant business.

For another thing, the sub was HUGE.

Not tall—HUGE.

As in, mega-ripped.

He wore a polo shirt and khakis—both of which were about to bust at the seams because of the muscles they attempted to contain. The right sleeve of his polo shirt covered the top half of a tattoo. All I could see was a pitchfork or something. I didn't realize it then, but looking back, I'm almost certain the rest of the tattoo must have been a bald eagle holding not only the pitchfork but a rifle too. In other words, I'm pretty sure this guy had been a Navy Seal.

He held a grade book in front of him. When he opened his mouth to take roll, I fully expected his voice to boom like a pro wrestler's—but it didn't.

"Anderson, Nick," he said, his voice soft enough that I had to lean in from my spot in the back row to hear it.

The guy in front of the class squinted at Nick for a second or two: "I'll do my best to attach your name and your face, Mr. Anderson."

He continued to go down the list of names alphabetically, each time squinting for a few seconds at the person who said, "Here."

When he said, "Hueller, Patrick," I could barely hear him.

Eventually he said, "Sanderson, Stu," but no one answered. He raised his voice, "Mr. Sanderson, are you here?"

"Move on, man," Chad Logan said. "Stu's MIA as usual."

He said it so casually that I think he was trying to prove he wasn't intimidated by the guy's muscles. Who Chad was trying to prove this to, I'm not sure. The guy reading roll? The rest of the class? Himself? Maybe all three.

The sub stood there, squinting at Chad, and then he said, "Who here knows what a euphemism is?"

No one raised a hand.

"It's when you say something that means something else," Clara Berns said.

It was the first time I'd heard her bother to speak in class. Which made her even more awesome. She only decided to speak when she could contribute actual information; otherwise, she let others do the talking.

"That's a good start, Ms. Berns," the guy said. "Can anyone give me an example?"

No one raised a hand.

"In that case, I've got one," the man said. He went to the chalkboard and leaned his attendance list against the blackboard. When he picked up a piece of chalk, I thought it would get pulverized between his fingers, but it didn't. The guy raised his hand to write and the sleeve of his polo moved up a little. I saw more of his tattoo. There were talons, and wings.

PASSED AWAY, the man wrote on the board.

"Here's another one," he said.

CROAK, he wrote.

"And another one," he said.

WORM FOOD.

He turned to us.

"If these are euphemisms," he said, "what are they euphemisms of?"

"Death," Chad Logan shouted out with a weird amount of enthusiasm.

"Exactly," the guy said. "So why do we use them? Why don't we just say someone died?"

"It's not as funny," Chad said.

"Maybe," the guy said. "But why do we need to be funny about death? Is death funny to you, Mr. Logan?"

The question sounded like a challenge. Chad didn't say anything.

The guy stopped squinting at Chad and looked at all of us. "The reason we use euphemisms is because sometimes we can't bear not to. Sometimes the only way we can communicate our grief is by downplaying it. There are times," the guy told us, "that the only way we can talk about something important is by talking about something else."

It was strange. His voice gained intensity as it lowered in volume. Even the kids in the front row had to lean in to hear him.

The guy went to the blackboard again and he erased the list of euphemisms. In their place, he wrote something else. As he wrote he said the words out loud.

For Whom The Bell Tolls

No man is an island,
Entire of itself.
Each is a piece of the continent,
A part of the main.

If a clod be washed away by the sea,
Europe is the less.
As well as if a promontory were.
As well as if a manner of thine own
Or of thine friend's were.
Each man's death diminishes me,
For I am involved in mankind.
Therefore, send not to know
For whom the bell tolls,
It tolls for thee.

He turned to us. "These words were written a long time ago by a guy named John Donne," he said. "Can anyone spot the euphemisms for death?"

"Exactly," the sub said after we'd come up with a few. "One possible interpretation of Donne's words is that, in the end, we're all the same. Dirt clod or big rock, we all get washed away by the sea. We all die. So there's no point, really, in trying to make our lives unique."

He stopped there.

"Is that what he's saying?" Justin Richards asked.

"What do you think, Mr. Richards?"

Justin looked pretty defeated, and I almost raised my hand. *No*, I wanted to say, *I don't think that's what he's saying.* In fact, he seemed to be saying the exact opposite. But I couldn't quite put it into words what I thought Donne was trying to communicate.

"Tell you what," the sub said. "Let's table that question for now. Maybe we'll get back to it later. For now, hopefully we can agree that what we say and how we say it are important—or should be. Euphemisms demonstrate that we have the ability to talk about something even by talking about something else." He grabbed his grade book from the chalkboard. "So, this Mr. Sanderson," he said. "Is he really missing in action, as one of you suggested? Keep in mind that that's a military term, and it's used to indicate that a soldier's well-being is unknown. He or she might be captured, or fleeing for life, or dead."

All of a sudden he was getting choked up. I swear. For the second time that school year, a huge behemoth of a guy began tearing up. But the sub's tears were different than Assistant Principal Baker's. They were somehow more restrained and more intense. He cleared his throat and turned away from us. A single teardrop rolled down the side of his cheek.

"Mr. Sanderson," he said again. "Can I get a report on his status?"

"Present and accounted for."

The voice was Stu's, and it came from behind the man.

It came from the podium.

The first thing I saw was Stu's hand. Then the rest of his body followed. Stu unfolded his limbs and stepped away from the podium.

"Glad you made it, Mr. Sanderson," the sub said.

"Call me Mr. Island," Stu said.

The guy squinted some more as he considered Stu's request. "I'd rather not," he said finally. "But I'll call you Dirt Clod, if you'd like."

Now it was Stu's turn to consider the offer. "Dirt Clod," he said, "yeah, I like the sound of that." Then he said, "And what are we supposed to call you?"

The sub did some more squinting.

"You can call me Mr. Bell," he finally said.

The Last Incredible Account of Dirt Clod and His Sidekick Bird Bones

Of course, I didn't know at the time that this would be Stu's last adventure. How could I? How could I have possibly predicted what was about to happen to my best friend?

Here's what I did know:

The Valentine's Day dance was only a week away, but no matter how many times Stu asked her, Clara refused to go with him. "Sorry, Dirt Clod," she finally told him, "I don't dance."

To which Stu asked, "What *do* you do?"

Clara didn't say anything. Instead, she grabbed his hand and wrote an address on it. Then she craned her neck back, looked Stu in the face, and said, "Be there right after school." She had taken three or four steps away before she yelled over her shoulder, "Patrick can come too. We could use his quickness."

I had no idea what that meant—use my quickness for what?—but Stu and I agreed there was only one way to find out.

Mom drove both of us to the address on Stu's hand. That day was the first warm day in months—well, it was above freezing, anyway—and it was a good thing too. If it had been colder, Stu might have frozen his face off. He was so tall that he had to stick his head out the window just to fit in the backseat. As Mom drove, I tried to ask him how he was doing—but the wind blasted his face too loudly for him to hear me.

I think we were both surprised when we figured out where we were going.

The Sports Bubble.

A big, white, inflatable dome that has different kinds of sport fields inside.

Mom told me to call her when we needed to get picked up, then drove away. Inside the dome we found a bunch of kids playing a game with a Frisbee. I later learned the game was called Ultimate—but I'd never heard of it back then. I don't remember which of us spotted Clara first. Instead of her usual dull-colored sweater and jeans, she wore a t-shirt and shorts.

Pink shorts.

After all this time imagining what her bare legs looked like, there they were right in front of me. And they were every bit as magnificent as I'd suspected.

Why on earth had she wanted to keep them hidden?

It was only after watching those awesome, toned, muscular calves for about five minutes that it occurred to me she wasn't wearing any shoes. None of them were.

I asked Stu if we should join their game (why else would Clara have invited us?), but for the first and only time I can remember, Stu chickened out. He told me he wasn't ready yet.

I asked him what he meant.

"They're all good, Bird Bones," he said. "The other players. They're all really good. If I want to impress Clara, I have to be good too."

I asked him, "If you don't want to play, what do you want to do?"

"Practice, dude."

By then he was already striding back to the turnstile.

We ended up back at Stu's house. He pulled himself up on top of the awning, went inside through his bedroom window, and—a few minutes later—came out the front door holding a Frisbee.

It didn't take long to see why Stu hadn't wanted to play Ultimate. To put it as gently as possible, he was completely pathetic at throwing a Frisbee.

Have you ever made what you think is a perfect paper airplane, but then you toss it in the air and it flutters a few times and nosedives right in front of you?

That's what Stu's Frisbee throws were like. We were playing on the street, and he kept backing up farther and farther. He'd take a few long steps for momentum, reach the Frisbee way back, swing it forward, release it . . . and then we'd both watch it wobble and crash land only a few yards in front of him.

I've never liked offering people advice when they don't ask for it. But after a watching Stu retrieve the Frisbee for about the millionth time, I couldn't stand it any longer. I told him to give me the Frisbee so he could see how I threw it.

Suddenly, as I offered him more pointers, he interrupted me.

"You're right, Bird Bones," he said. "If I'm going to impress Clara, it's not going to be by throwing the Frisbee. It's going to be by catching it."

Then he explained that his height advantage could make him unstoppable.

"Okay," I said, "but why are you taking off your shoes?"

It's true. He was untying his sneakers and pulling them off.

"Didn't you see the players at the bubble?" he asked. "None of them were wearing shoes." He peeled off his socks and threw them to the side of the street with his sneakers. Instantly, his toes and then the rest of his feet went white. After all, it was cold. Not as cold as it had been just a few weeks ago—the sun had thawed most of the ice on the street—but it was only February. Spring warmth was still at least a month away.

I tried to explain they were inside, playing on turf; we were outside, playing on the street. But Stu was already galloping down the road. He stopped like fifty yards away.

"Throw it really high, dude," he yelled.

I did. I reached back and flung the Frisbee as far and high as I possibly could.

Too high, it turned out.

Stu jumped and reached with both hands, but the Frisbee hit a wind current and sailed over his outstretched fingertips.

It continued to sail across the road and—what are the odds?—right into a sewer drain.

It was an accidental perfect shot. No skidding or anything. One moment the Frisbee was airborne, the next it was gone.

Stu crossed the street, knelt by the curb, and peered inside the drain.

"Sorry, man," I told him as I hustled over. "I think I have another Frisbee at home. We can—"

But Stu interrupted me. "I can see it, dude. It's right there." He looked over his shoulder at me. "Let's get it."

It was true that Stu had squeezed inside a podium. It was even true that he had squeezed inside an air vent.

But that was a big air vent, and this was a regular-sized sewer drain.

"Even you can't fit in there, Stu."

"No, Bird Bones. We won't go through here—we'll go through there." He pointed back to the road at a manhole cover.

I didn't understand. "What? How?"

"By taking the cover off, dude." He said it like it was obvious. "I bet those garden stakes would do the trick."

He pointed over my shoulder. I turned and looked at the yard across the street from Stu's house. It had a garden in the front yard. Well, it had a dirt patch in the front yard. It was still too cold for flowers.

Stu took a half dozen strides to make it to the "garden" and pull two stakes out of the partly frozen ground.

When he returned, he held out one of the stakes for me to take.

Looking back, it was here that I should have put my foot down. "No," I should have said, "this is a bad idea."

But I didn't do that—partly because I was interested to see what would happen next, and partly because I didn't think it would do any good. Stu had made up his mind, and there was no talking him out of it. This was a kid who once licked a frozen pole as a "magic trick." How was I supposed to stop him from trying to open a manhole cover?

We wedged the sticks into the cover and agreed to pull on the count of three.

"One . . ." Stu said, "two . . . three!"

We both pulled.

Instantly, the stake I was holding bent in half.

For some reason, though, Stu's didn't. Maybe he had a different angle, or more leverage, or maybe we mistimed our pulling. For all I knew, he might have had more practice lifting manhole covers. Whatever the reason, the cover moved. It lifted.

Which is when Stu slipped.

I watched him fall. And then I heard him scream.

Maybe scream isn't the right word. It was lower than that. He bellowed.

It wasn't a sound I'd ever heard before, and it took me a second to understand why he had made it.

His foot—his bare foot—was trapped underneath the manhole cover and the sewer opening.

That day, I performed two feats of strength I can't explain. This was one of those times. I honestly don't know how I did it—now that the cover was raised a little, it was more manageable, I guess—but I grabbed the cover and I yanked it off his foot. I watched the cover wobble, roll, and rest on the other side of the sewer hole.

Then I turned back to Stu.

He lay there on the street with his foot hanging over the sewer. It was covered in blood. He wasn't bellowing anymore. In fact, he was eerily quiet.

"Stu? Are you okay?"

He didn't say anything, but he sat up. He stared at his foot for a few seconds, and then he began to scoot forward.

"Stu—stop—what are you—"

He disappeared into the sewer.

I now realize he must have been in shock, but at the time I didn't know what to think or do. My brain and body felt paralyzed. Maybe I was in shock too.

I watched the whole thing and didn't move a muscle.

A voice said, "I got it, Bird Bones!"

I was standing a few feet from the sewer hole, too far away to look directly into it. But I could see the edge of the Frisbee. I took a few steps forward. There was Stu, standing on a ladder rung, holding up and waving the disc. I bent down to take it and said, "Good for you. Now will you please get out of there?"

Or I started to say that, but Stu pulled the Frisbee back before I could take it and said, "It's awesome down here, dude." He climbed the rest of the way down the ladder. "Let's go exploring."

Before I knew what was happening, I could hear the splash of his footsteps.

I should have called 9-1-1 right then, probably. Stu's foot had looked really bad—and now he was sloshing around in sewage water? I should have knocked on people's front doors until someone let me use their phone. (This was before kids had cell phones.) But the truth is that the thought never occurred to me. I heard Stu's sloshing and all I could think to do was follow him into the sewer.

As I climbed down the ladder, I listened to the sewage gush underneath me. Luckily, it wasn't as deep as I assumed. Stepping off the ladder, I landed in no more than four or five inches of liquid. Which isn't to say it wasn't plenty gross. And plenty creepy. The liquid was surprisingly warm, but that just made it grosser. The sewer was pitch black, and part of me was glad that it was. That way, I didn't have to see what I was walking in. The only evidence I had that this wasn't a stream of water was the smell. Gas. Rot. More gas. I tried to breathe only through my mouth.

"Stu?"

My voice echoed like his footsteps had.

"Here, dude," he replied.

I couldn't see him and, because of the echoing, I had to guess which way his voice had come from. I only knew I'd guessed right when my nose collided with his back.

"Stu, seriously. We should get back."

He didn't reply or in any way acknowledge he'd heard me. Instead, he started rambling. "I bet this place goes all over the town. We could go anywhere and no one would even know we're there. Seriously. Wanna go underneath the school? Or the bank? Or the prison?"

His words came faster and faster. He sounded delirious. Like some sort of insane tour guide.

We splashed along the sewer.

"Stu—" I tried.

But he just kept talking: "or anywhere or wherever or however or whyever we want and no one realizes anything because they think we're gone and . . . "

I'm not going to lie, it was weird. Freaky weird. But I also didn't want him to stop talking, because his voice was the only way I knew he was still in front of me.

The only light we had came from the sewer grates. As we passed a grate, a shaft of sky would shine down on us and I could see Stu for a few seconds. He would stand up straight for a few strides before hunching over again as we entered another tunnel.

The brief moments of light allowed me to see other things too. Cockroaches dropped from the tops of tunnel walls. Rats' eyes flared white and then went black again. Chunks of stuff (dirt, I told myself, it's only dirt) washed by our feet.

That's when I noticed Stu was limping severely. He couldn't lift his injured foot out of the sewage. As we passed another grate I saw the trail of blood flowing behind him.

At some point, in between grates, Stu stopped babbling. I was just about to yell his name again when I bumped into him. There was a splash. A much bigger splash than his footfalls had been making.

"Stu?" I said—but he didn't answer me.

I reached for him. When all I felt was air, I realized he must have fallen.

More accurately, I must have knocked him over.

Before I knew it, I was on my knees in the water, still blindly reaching for my friend. With one hand, I found what I thought were the backs of his knees. With the other, I found what must have been his waist.

This was my second impossible feat of strength.

I picked him up.

From a kneeling position I heaved and hoisted and got to my feet. I staggered in the direction I thought we had come—though in the dark I couldn't be certain.

I kept staggering until I got to another sewer grate. Then I screamed, "HELP!"

I screamed and screamed and screamed.

I screamed until I couldn't scream any longer. I screamed until I couldn't carry Stu another second.

My arms gave out. I heard Stu splash on the sewer floor again.

But no one came to our rescue.

I looked toward the sewer floor and let my eyes re-adjust to the darkness. Stu's body lay face up and motionless. Sewage water streamed past his ears.

Was he dead?

No. I found his pulse.

He must have fainted.

"Stu? Stu! Say something, Stu!"

He opened his eyes.

"What are we still doing down here, Bird Bones?" He didn't sound at all worried. Far from it. He was in good spirits. "Let's get out of here."

"When you put it like that," I said, "I guess you're right."

We both started to get up.

"Huh," Stu said.

"What?"

"I can't move my foot."

"Are you serious?"

"No worries, dude. I'll hop my way to freedom."

"Where are we going to hop to?"

"Back where we came from, Bird Bones."

"Do you know which way that is?"

Stu thought about it. "Negatory." He scratched his chin, nodded, and hopped away from the light pouring in from the sewer grate. "Over here, Bird Bones. We're saved."

I walked over. He'd found a ladder. I watched him try to climb it. A few seconds later, he splashed to the ground. "All my strength seems to be gone."

He said this almost cheerfully, as though he found his numb-footed, weakened state to be interesting.

"I think we should probably wait here until someone comes," I said.

"Glad to hear you say that, dude. Because I'm getting a little lightheaded."

Then he fainted again.

Or maybe he slept.

I thought for a while he might be in a coma because he didn't come to when I tried yelling, "HELP!" a few more times.

But I don't think you can snore while in a coma, can you?

Finally, after what felt like hours, someone did come. "Hello?" the someone said. All I could see was the someone's nose and mouth in the sewer grate "Who's down there?"

I didn't know how to answer her question. What did she want, our names? Ages? Physical descriptions?

"Who's UP there?" I asked.

"Meg, sir. I'm a waiter at Neighbors Bar and Grill. What can I get for you?"

Her voice was casual. Friendly. It was almost as if she was asking us what we wanted to drink.

"Can you call the police?" I said.

"You got it, sir. I'll be right back with your order. I mean, I'll be right back."

Stu suddenly sat up.

"Bring some buffalo wings while you're at it," he said.

"Right away, sir," she said.

In a few minutes sirens and lights blared through the sewer grate. The cops or paramedics used a giant magnet to remove the manhole cover, then sent a guy down to get Stu. When he saw Stu's size, he asked for backup. Not just anyone could carry Stu, I guess.

The sewer we emerged from was in an alley behind the restaurant. By now Stu had been placed on a stretcher. The EMTs were about to wheel him to an ambulance, but Stu said, "Hold up a sec, dudes. I put in an order for some wings."

They had no time to argue. Right on cue, Meg—our loyal waitress—rushed out of the alley with a basket of wings.

"Sorry, sir, I forgot the celery and the ranch dressing," she said. She sounded flustered. "So the wings are free."

They let me ride in the ambulance with Stu, but then I had to wait for him in the lobby. The more I thought about it, the more certain I was that we were going to get suspended for all of this.

Or in even worse trouble.

Legal trouble.

I mean, there's no way it's legal to remove a manhole cover, let alone walk around in the sewer.

I actually thought Stu was the lucky one. They'd probably feel sorry for him because of his bloody foot— but me? If you wanted people's sympathy, it was better to be an injured criminal than a healthy one.

I don't know how long I waited in the lobby, but finally the doctor came out to talk to me. Or that's what I thought he was doing. It turned out he was coming out to talk to the woman sitting next to me. Somehow, I hadn't even noticed her presence, despite the fact that she was tall. Teeteringly so. Even while sitting she was as tall as the doctor who stood in front of her.

"Ms. Sanderson?" the doctor said.

She looked up from the magazine she was reading.

"You're . . . Stu's *mom*?" I blurted out.

After all this time, I was finally going to meet one of Stu's parents!

"Stu's aunt," the woman said.

Oh. Right. His aunt was technically taking care of him while his parents were overseas somewhere, doing military things. Stu was always pretty vague about what military things they were doing exactly, but my imagination wasn't. I already imagined them as superspies who spoke multiple languages and knew even more martial arts. After all, they couldn't just be normal people—not *Stu's parents*. Still, I couldn't help noticing that, despite her excessive height, his aunt looked pretty normal. And by normal I mean normally middle-aged. Her body looked a little stiffened and brittle with age. I certainly couldn't imagine her pulling off Stu-like feats, let alone ninja-ing her way across the world as I'd imagined his parents doing.

"Who are you?" Stu's aunt said.

"Stu's best friend," I said.

"I have bad news," the doctor said.

"Oh, forgive me," Stu's aunt said. She closed her magazine, stood up and began walking away. "I didn't mean to intrude."

The doctor looked confused. I'm sure I did too.

"Intrude? I've come out here specifically to talk with you," the doctor explained.

Now it was Stu's aunt's turn to be confused. "Why would you want to share difficult news with me when you have his best friend here? The only time I see Stu is on holidays. This young man sees him every day. You have my permission, young man, to do whatever you need to do to help Stu."

With that, she strolled away, one long, brittle stride at a time. I honestly wasn't sure whether the young man she was referring to was me or the doctor.

In any case, as she walked away, I couldn't help thinking: *She's just like Stu. Same weird way of reasoning that was, in the end, totally logical.*

The doctor must have agreed, because he went ahead and told me the bad news.

Remember when I said Stu was the lucky one?

I was wrong.

Stu had an infection, the doctor said. A bad infection.

How bad?

They were going to have to amputate his foot.

I wanted to go see him right away, but he was already being prepped for surgery. Finally, several hours later, I was given permission to visit Stu's room. But by then I'd changed my mind. I didn't want to see him at all. I mean, what was I going to say to him?

"I'm sorry to hear about your foot"?

"Better luck next time"?

"Everything will turn out all right"?

Weak, lame, and untrue. Things clearly were not going to turn out all right—everything was not fine. Not for his foot, anyway.

I have to admit, I was feeling plenty guilty too.

"I'm sorry I couldn't scream louder," I knew I should say. "I'm sorry I couldn't save you before the infection in your foot got really bad."

At least that apology had some truth to it.

A nurse guided me into the hospital room. Stu was lying on a white bed, partly reclined. One leg was tucked under the white blanket. The other one rested on top.

The one on top was nothing but a stump. It wasn't just his foot that had been removed. Almost everything below the knee was gone.

The stump had been bandaged in layers of gauze.

"Did you hear the good news, Bird Bones?"

I looked up to find Stu grinning at me. "Huh?"

"I get to have a robotic leg!" he said. "It's like when Luke Skywalker gets the mechanical hand!"

"Huh?" I said again.

"Check this out!" He flung something, Frisbee-style, in my direction. It fluttered through the air before I caught it. It was a magazine. A magazine full of different models of prosthetic limbs.

Or, as he referred to them for the rest of the time I was in the room, robo replicas.

"I like the robo rep on page 36," he said. "But I'm open to suggestions."

So, yeah—there's no denying it: Stu's psychotic.

But he might also be my hero.

(Just in case some of you are wondering: yes, I did get suspended. Stu and I both did. But the truth is I didn't really think about school, anyway. Stu spent those two weeks—plus several more months after that—recovering from the amputation. I spent those two weeks visiting him in the hospital.

I should also say, I suppose, that despite Stu's attempt at non-stop cheerfulness, the amputation wasn't all fun and games. Not even close. A lot of the time Stu was folded up like origami, bellowing in pain. But Stu didn't want me to see that, and he certainly wouldn't want me to dwell on it here. That's why I kept it in parentheses. It would have been irresponsible, I think, to suggest Stu was totally fine—but it would also be disrespectful to totally ignore the way he would want his story told.)

It didn't take long for people to start visiting Stu at the hospital. Most of the students only stayed long enough to drop off a card or flowers or to offer Stu a high five. As much as students liked Stu, they seemed to have difficulty maintaining a conversation with him. How do you talk about life with someone who seemed so much bigger than life?

Mr. Bell, our substitute teacher, didn't have that problem, because unlike others he was able to talk with Stu as a peer. It's weird how someone you've only met once can turn out to be just as important as people you've known your whole life. I'm not exactly sure why Stu and Mr. Bell understood each other so well; maybe it had something to do with Stu's military background.

"Well, what do you think?" Stu asked him. "Can I be called an island yet?"

Mr. Bell squinted at him for a second. He pressed his hands together in a way that made his muscular arms strain his shirtsleeves. Finally he said, "No man is an island, Mr. Dirt Clod."

Stu loved it.

When Stu got his prosthetic leg, he said, "How about now, Mr. Bell? I'm not just a man anymore. I'm part robot. Can a robot be an island?"

Mr. Bell just shook his head and reminded him how important his physical therapy sessions would be.

Ms. Gribbs showed up too. She kept looking at his stump as though she expected the foot to grow back any second. Maybe she figured that if Stu could dematerialize and rematerialize, his foot could do the same thing.

In any case, she was really happy to see Stu. "When I heard about the accident," she said, "I was so afraid I was going to lose you too."

Lose you too? I thought. Maybe she really had lost a student before.

Or maybe she was just—to use the technical term—utterly off her rocker.

Clara Berns showed up too. Several times.

Then, one night, she showed up at my front door.

Wearing a dress.

A blue-sequined dress that was just short enough to show off her toned legs.

She'd asked Stu to go to the Valentine's Day dance first, but he'd (in her words) "wimped out." We both knew he must have been having one of his bad days. I imagined him folded up like origami, bellowing in pain.

Anyway, when Stu couldn't go, he convinced her to ask me instead.

Had he known all this time how I felt about her?

Yet again, Stu proved he was the greatest friend ever.

And if you think I had too much pride to be Clara's fallback plan, you're wrong.

I decided not to remind her that she didn't like dancing. Neither of us liked it very much, actually—except for the slow songs.

While we slow danced, I finally asked her why she wears pants all the time.

"They probably wouldn't want me showing up naked from the waist down," she said.

"No, I mean *long* pants. Why don't you ever wear shorts at school?"

"Because," she said, "my legs never seemed like anyone else's business at this school."

She explained that her parents had transferred her away from her old school without her permission. "They said Babbling Brook was a better school or whatever." But they didn't seem to care she was losing all her friends from her old school. "That's who you saw me playing Ultimate with." Up until this year, she told me, she'd played more than Ultimate. She'd been on the varsity soccer and track teams at her old school (as a seventh grader!). "My parents didn't care about that, either." They wanted her to spend more time reading, so she decided to give them what they wanted. They never said the books had to be related to class. "Besides," she said, "what's the fun of sports if you're not with your friends?" When she arrived at Babbling Brook, no one seemed interested in having anything to do with her, and she wasn't about to beg.

"I—er, I mean we, Stu and me—we want to have something to do with you," I said.

"I want to have something to do with you guys too," she said.

Then she bent at the waist and kissed me on the cheek.

I could still feel my cheek buzzing the next morning when I entered Stu's hospital room.

The first thing he said to me was, "She kissed you, didn't she? Well guess what, she kissed me too."

He pointed to his cheek like I'd still be able see the imprint of her lips. His skin must have been buzzing too.

Several months later, Stu finally got out of the hospital.

To celebrate, we went to a baseball game. This was before our team, the Twins, had an outdoor baseball stadium, so we decided to drive to Milwaukee to watch the Brewers instead. Stu had been cooped up since February; he wanted to feel the sun on his face.

Clara came too. The two of us sat in the backseat. Stu sat shotgun. He needed to scooch his seat way back in order to be comfortable. That meant I had to take the middle seat in back. After all, I had the shortest legs. Not that I minded: sitting in the middle seat meant I could spend the whole trip with my hip and knee pressed against Clara's.

Oh, and guess who was driving?

Ms. Gribbs—that's who.

Basically every adult we knew had volunteered to take us to the game, but Stu gave Ms. Gribbs the go-ahead. He said they'd really bonded over the last few months. Frankly, this surprised me. I'd never witnessed any of this bonding.

After we'd been on the road a few hours we found ourselves stuck in a huge traffic jam. We might as well have been sitting in a parking lot. A half hour later we'd moved maybe twenty feet.

Stu announced he was bored.

"Sorry to hear that, Stu," I said. "What do you want us to do about it?"

"We should play Frisbee, dude."

Now he had Clara's attention.

"Where?" I asked. "In the car?"

"No, Bird Bones. Outside."

Now he had Ms. Gribbs's attention. "You are not to get out of this car," she half said, half shrieked.

"Don't worry, Ms. Gribbs," I reassured her. "We don't even have a Frisbee."

"Yes we do," Stu said. "The one you threw into the sewer."

I tried to jog my memory. Did he have the Frisbee the whole time we were in the sewer? Did he have it with him on the stretcher? In the ambulance? In the hospital? I was reasonably certain he didn't. Had he gone back in the sewer to retrieve it? I imagined him sneaking out of the hospital and crutching his way into the sewer. It was hard to believe, but I couldn't put it past him.

"I'm in," Clara said.

Ms. Gribbs shrieked again.

"It's in my bag behind you, Bird Bones," Stu said. "Do you mind reaching for it?"

Ms. Gribbs's car was a hatchback, and I reached into the trunk behind me.

I unzipped the bag. I wasn't sold on the idea of leaving the car to play Frisbee on the side of the road, but I had to admit I was curious to see the Frisbee.

I was reaching behind me, so I couldn't see inside the bag very well. I felt for the Frisbee but didn't locate it at first.

"Are you sure it's there, Stu?"

"Dig around, dude. You'll find it."

I did dig around, but I didn't find it.

Instead, I found myself touching something different. Something cold (*frozen*, I know now). Something definitely NOT plastic.

I pulled it out of the bag.

"Stu—what the . . . ?"

Stu looked at me, grinning, and said, "It's my foot, dude."

Ms. Gribbs shrieked even louder. Clara said, "Cool!"

"I can see that." Actually, it was more than his foot. It was his ankle and most of his calf too. I only looked at the toes long enough to observe they were crusted with blood. I couldn't smell anything—probably because it was still frozen—but I wasn't going to take any chances. I breathed through my mouth like I had done in the sewer. "What are you . . . how did you get it?"

"I asked the nurse."

He said it like it was obvious.

"And that worked?"

"Of course not," he said.

"So you stole it," I said.

"Can someone really steal his own body part, dude?"

He reached back and took his foot from me.

With the other hand, he removed his robo leg. I thought for a second he was going to try to jam his foot back in place, but he didn't.

He opened his door.

Ms. Gribbs kept right on shrieking.

There was Stu, hopping from one car to another and tapping his frozen, severed foot against their windows. His voice boomed as usual.

"Excuse me," he told one car. "Could you help me put this back on?"

"Pardon me," he said to another. "Is this your foot or mine? I wouldn't want to take the wrong foot."

"My apologies," he said to another car. He was way down the road now, but his booming voice made it to our car loud and clear. "Could I borrow your spare tire? My own mode of transportation fell off."

He held up his foot again.

It was pretty clear, right then, that Stu was indeed well on his way to becoming legendary. And that maybe his adventures weren't over after all. Maybe, indeed, they were just beginning.

About the Author

Along with being a writer, Patrick Hueller is short. If you've read *Stu Stories*, you know that Patrick's shortness is one of the reasons his friend Stuart Sanderson calls him "Bird Bones." There are a couple fun facts about Patrick. For instance, he has an identical twin brother, Andy Hueller. Andy's a writer for Cedar Fort too. He's short too. Believe it or not, Patrick's wife also has an identical twin. Patrick's wife is also a writer. Patrick's not sure whether she considers herself (and her twin sister) to be short. That's pretty much all the fun facts about Patrick. He's pretty boring. That's why he doesn't write about himself.
Instead, he writes about Stu. Stu has an endless list of fun facts. For starters, he's not short. Not at all. In fact, he's the least short person Patrick has ever known. And the least boring.

You can learn more about Patrick and, more important, about Stu at Patrick's website: patrickhueller.com.

0 26575 19554 5